No More Nasty

by Amy MacDonald

Pictures by Cat Bowman Smith

Melanie Kroupa Books
Farrar Straus Giroux
New York

Text copyright © 2001 by Amy MacDonald
Illustrations copyright © 2001 by Cat Bowman Smith
All rights reserved
Distributed in Canada by Douglas & McIntyre Ltd.
Printed in the United States of America
Designed by Jennifer Browne
First edition, 2001
10   9   8   7   6   5

Library of Congress Cataloging-in-Publication Data

MacDonald, Amy.
    No more nasty / by Amy MacDonald ; illustrated by Cat
Bowman Smith.— 1st ed.
        p. cm.
    Summary: When Simon's Great Aunt Matilda becomes
the substitute teacher for his unruly fifth-grade class,
her unique way of looking at things gives the students
a new perspective on learning.
    ISBN 0-374-35529-0
    [1. Substitute teachers—Fiction. 2. Teacher-student
relationships—Fiction. 3. Schools—Fiction. 4. Great-
aunts—Fiction. 5. Humorous stories.] I. Smith, Cat
Bowman, ill.   II. Title.

PZ7.M1463 Nn 2001
[Fic]—dc21
                                          00-31687

For Jeremy, my best reader, and Alex
(he knows why)

Biggs Bites the Dust

Where was Mrs. Biggs? Simon glanced at the clock over the door. It was the same kind of round, white clock you saw in every classroom you ever went into. It said 9:05.

No one had ever known Mrs. Biggs to be late—for class, for anything. She was the kind of person, thought Simon, who would be on time for her own execution by firing squad. And then she would give the firing squad a lecture for being thirty seconds late. Her last official act.

"Seventeen million," said Sebastian to Simon.

"Hunh?"

"Seventeen million poisonous snakes," Sebastian repeated patiently. "In the snake pit."

"Yeah," said Simon, returning to his work. He was writing, and Sebastian was illustrating, the second installment of a comic book series they called X-Boys. This issue was called "Big Bites Back," and they had just come to the part where a certain "Mrs. Big" falls into a snake pit.

"She survives, of course," said Simon, "because when the snakes bite her, *they* all die."

"Of course," said Sebastian.

"But," added Simon, "I've just figured out how she *does* die. In the next issue, 'Big Bites the Dust': execution by firing squad."

"Great idea."

"But I doubt even a firing squad—" He was interrupted when a photon missile struck him in the ear.

Simon looked around. He wasn't the only one taking advantage of Mrs. Biggs's absence.

Jimmy had stolen some paper rocket ships from Raggie's desk—Raggie himself was wandering the halls somewhere—and was launching them from Mrs. Biggs's desk. Ethan was trying to shoot them down using the latest photon missile technology (okay, paper clips launched from a rubber band).

And Mindy and Mandy and Mollie had formed a circle with their desks. Mollie was listening to music on headphones. The other two were writing a story called "The Three Little Biggs." They were reading aloud the part where an old wolf, freezing with cold and dying of hunger, knocks on the door of the first Little Bigg. He begs to be allowed in from the snowstorm. "You can't come in," says the first Little Bigg. "You spoke without raising your hand. You don't have a hall pass. Where's your permission slip? Bad wolf."

Bix was leading a hoop-shooting contest, using wadded-up pieces of paper and Mrs. Biggs's wastebasket, perched high atop two desks that he'd stacked next to the door.

Behind Bix, Mario sat with his head on his desk, fast asleep, as usual, despite the chaos.

And Julie was at the blackboard, entertaining the rest of the class with her extremely accurate imitation of their teacher. Julie was a large girl with expressive, dark eyes, and an unsettling habit of casting sidelong glances at grown-ups as if she didn't believe a word they said. She was also a deadly mimic. Arms folded on her chest, she was now addressing Moses Haskell in an acid voice. Moses, a big, shy, dreamy boy with a stutter, had been a favorite target of Mrs. Biggs's sarcasm.

"Think hard, Moses," Julie was saying, peering at him over a pair of glasses that she'd pushed down to the tip of her nose. "Two plus two equals . . . ?"

"Uh, f-four?" said Moses, playing along.

"Light dawns over Marblehead!" said Julie, with a grand gesture. Marblehead being the name of a neighboring town, this had been one of Mrs. Biggs's favorite expressions. "Thank you, Mr. Einstein!" Julie gave him her nastiest smile and removed her glasses, just as Mrs. Biggs always did when she wanted to make a point. The kids around her burst out laughing.

At that very moment Herbert J. Bickle, their principal, opened the door and walked in. He was holding the missing Raggie firmly by the shoulder, and he had only a microsecond to take in the chaos in the classroom before one of Bix's just-launched "basketballs" bounced off his forehead and landed in the wastebasket.

"Yesss!" shouted Bix. "A three-pointer! A thirty-pointer!"

"Children!" cried Mr. Bickle, rubbing his head. "This is . . . please!"

The class suddenly seemed to realize just exactly who Mr. Bickle was. Something resembling silence fell. Students, desks, chairs, and wastebaskets slowly found their way back to their proper places.

Julie stuck up her hand. "Where is Mrs. Biggs?" she asked, without waiting to be called on. "She's late."

Mr. Bickle ignored her. He was a small, dapper man with white hair and a neat bow tie. When the class was finally silent and seated, he cleared his throat, and his face assumed a grave expression. "I have some bad . . . I'm sorry to say . . . it's very sad . . . for you," he began. Simon prepared himself for everyone's favorite guessing game: trying to figure out just what the heck the principal was trying to say. Mr. Bickle was famously unable to finish a sentence. "Mrs. Biggs won't be . . . that is, your teacher will not . . . in other words, she has decided to take early retirement."

"She quit?" asked Julie, managing to say in two small words what had taken Mr. Bickle a whole paragraph. Mr. Bickle nodded.

"Well, I wouldn't put it exactly . . . It would be more accurate to . . . um . . . Correct."

"Yesss!" shouted Jimmy and Ethan. They leaped from their seats and punched the air, while the rest of the class cheered. Even Simon leaned back in his chair and let out a huge sigh. But Mr. Bickle resumed.

"And so"—then, louder—"*and so,* for the last five weeks

5

of school you will have . . . of course we have had to hire . . . at least I'm hoping . . . should have been here by now—"

"A substitute?" asked Julie.

"All *right*!" whooped the class.

"Who's it gonna be? Mr. Croker?" That was Julie again. She could do a very good imitation of all the usual substitute teachers—and there had been many— but Simon especially enjoyed the way she did Mr. Croker, a man with a strong overbite and absolutely no sense of discipline. His day generally ended with more than half the students being sent to Mr. Bickle's office.

"Yeah, who?" clamored the students.

"I, well, that is," said Mr. Bickle. He looked at his watch and cleared his throat again. "Ahem. Which is to say, we've had a little trouble . . . It was very short notice to . . . None of the usual teachers could . . . But we did manage to find a . . . although she seems to be a bit late. Perhaps she got . . ."

There was a knock on the classroom door. The principal opened it and stepped outside. Simon could hear the sounds of murmured conversation. Then, strong and clear, came a voice that was strangely familiar to Simon Maxwell:

"Of course I am. I *always* try to be at least fifteen minutes late. Makes things far more interesting—don't you think?"

Then the door opened, and in walked Simon's great-aunt Matilda.

Death, Where Is Thy Sting?

Simon slid down in his chair until just his head was visible above the desktop. Aunt Matilda! This couldn't be happening to him. That could not be his great-aunt standing at the front of the classroom with Mr. Bickle. He opened his eyes and peeked over his desk. Yes, it was. It was Aunt Mattie. Aunt Mattie in her huge hat with fruit and flowers on it. Aunt Mattie in her orange flowered dress and apron.

Simon slid even lower in his chair. Maybe she won't see me, he thought. Maybe she won't recognize me.

From this position, Simon could see Aunt Mattie's feet. He noted with dismay that she had one high-top basketball sneaker, and one shiny brown lace-up boot. Straw and bits of mud clung to both feet, and from Matilda herself there wafted the unmistakable odor of horse and barn. It was an odor that under any other circumstances would have filled Simon with joy, for he recently had spent a deliriously happy two weeks at Aunt Mattie's farm, most of it in the barn or with the horses.

Mr. Bickle was still talking.

"... so, class, will you please welcome, this is Mrs., um, Mrs.—"

"—Mrs. Maxwell," said Aunt Matilda helpfully.

"Yes. Mrs. ... Now class, I want you to ... and I'm sure you will be on your very best ... because if you're not, I'll be seeing you in my office, and ..." He came to a halting halt, and turned to Aunt Matilda. "Mrs. Biggs left a complete lesson plan that you ... and detailed information about all the students who ..." He handed her a package. Then, having run out of things to say, or having finished not finishing his things to say, he wished her luck and left.

Aunt Mattie stood at the front of the room. She surveyed the class. The class surveyed her. "Well," said Matilda at last. "And how does all your corporosity seem to gashiate?"

The class looked blankly back at her. No one knew the correct response to such an odd question, except for Simon, and he wasn't about to open his mouth. In fact, no one said a thing, or even blinked, except for Simon, who slowly closed both eyes and hoped the whole thing would go away. And in a funny way, it did. For when he closed his eyes it was suddenly spring and he was back at Matilda's farm.

It had been the best two weeks of his life. Something had happened to him during that visit—what it was he couldn't say—but after he returned to Mrs. Biggs's class, he felt different. He *was* different. For the first time in his life he had gotten into trouble for talking back to a teacher. A simple thing, really. Mrs. Biggs had been in the middle of chewing Jimmy out, trying to embarrass him for getting a math problem wrong on the blackboard. Jimmy was no friend of Simon's—just the opposite, in fact—but without much thinking about what he was doing, Simon had stood up and corrected Mrs. Biggs. Jimmy, he pointed out, had gotten the answer *right*. She, Mrs. Biggs, had gotten it *wrong*. Shocked by back talk in one she had always trusted to behave perfectly, Mrs. Biggs had sent him to the principal's office for the first time in his life. He went, covered in glory and detention slips.

Despite what Jimmy and his friends thought, Simon had not really been a teacher's pet. He didn't like

Mrs. Biggs any more than the other kids did. She was downright nasty: rude, sarcastic, and happiest when humiliating the poorer students. It was just that Simon had hated the thought of getting into trouble. He'd rather have died than have to sit in the chair outside the principal's office, with everyone looking at him. He had straight A's, no detentions—and no friends.

But after that episode, Jimmy had seemed to change his mind about Simon. They hadn't become friends, but a sort of truce was established. Because Jimmy had been held back a year, and was bigger than all the other boys, they tended to do whatever he did. So life got easier for Simon. Even Julie looked at him with new respect. And Simon knew that in some strange way he owed it all to Aunt Mattie.

And now this had to happen. Simon opened his eyes again. There she stood at the front of the class, as real as porridge and twice as embarrassing.

"Well, no one's corporosity seems to be gashiating at all," said Matilda, unworried by the silent class. "And now, what should we do first?"

With a start of dismay Simon saw Ethan loading half a paper clip onto his rubber band. He gave Simon a wink and launched the photon missile at the school bell just above Mattie's head. It hit with a resounding clang.

"Goodness me!" said Aunt Mattie. "Are we under attack?"

"No," said Jimmy, standing up. "That's the recess bell."

Simon looked at his classmates. They were all playing along, putting away their books and pretending it

10

was recess. He sighed. His class had a reputation for destroying substitute teachers. They'd even made it into a sport: Sink the Sub.

Simon knew his Aunt Mattie had a will of iron—little would you guess it behind that cloud of white hair—but even Aunt Mattie couldn't withstand this class. Could she? No, they'd eat her alive. And then spit out the bones.

"Recess already?" asked Aunt Mattie. "Is that the schedule?"

Julie put up her hand.

"Generally speaking," said Julie seriously, "we have morning recess from now until 9:45. Then we have free time until lunch. After lunch we have lunch recess. And at 2:30 it's time to go home."

Matilda gave her a long look.

"Generally speaking," added Julie.

Jimmy's hand shot up.

"Except some days we have gym instead of free time," he said. "Or art."

"Yeah," added Ethan. "And except tomorrow. Tomorrow there are no classes, so you won't have to come to school at all. Mr. Bickle asked us to remind you about that. It's like a, a—"

"A no-school day?" said Matilda, helpfully.

"Yeah, that's it. A no-school day, for some reason I can't think of right now."

"Perhaps it's national Sucker the Substitute Day?" asked Matilda.

"Yeah, that's it," said Ethan. "Something like that."

He shrugged. "Oh, well," he said to the slumbering Mario. "It was worth a try." He poked Mario in the ribs. "Right, Mario?"

Mario jerked awake. "What?" he said. "Where?"

"Now, children," said Matilda sternly, "if you are going to try to pull the wool over my eyes, I expect you to do a lot better than that. Let's see a little creative persiflage, at least. Do I look as if I was born yesterday?"

"No, ma'am," said Julie with her most sincere expression. "You look like you were born a long, *long* time ago."

No one laughed. Instead, there was a brief, dense silence, while the class waited to see what would happen. Simon covered his eyes.

"I was," said Matilda with a smile. "And I'll thank you all to keep that in mind. Now then, as I was saying, where do we start?"

The class let out a long, disappointed sigh. Most of them, Simon realized, were not only expecting Matilda to zap Julie—they were hoping for it. Even Julie looked disappointed. At last Mario spoke.

"You have to take attendance," he said listlessly. Then yawned.

"I do? Why?" asked Matilda.

"Well . . ." Mario shifted in his seat. "I dunno. So you know who's here. And who's not. And who's late. You write it down."

"All right, then," said Matilda. Inside the package Mr. Bickle had given her was one of those black grading books. On the first page was a list of all the students in the class. But Matilda put the book down and took out a notepad and pencil. She looked brightly about the room.

"Everyone who's here, please raise your hands." The whole class raised their hands. "Good. Everyone's here," she said, writing carefully on the pad. "Now, everyone who is *not* here, please raise your hands." No one raised a hand. "Good. No one's not here." She wrote some more notes on the pad. While she was looking down, Bix launched a last basketball at the trash can.

Matilda looked up. "Was anyone late this morning?" No one said a word. "Nobody? No one at all?"

Julie put up her hand.

"Oh, good. You were late," said Matilda. "I was beginning to give up hope." She spoke as she jotted down on her pad. "One person late."

"No," said Julie. "I wasn't late. I was going to say that *you* were late."

Simon held his breath. Julie was the class wise guy, but if she had said that to Mrs. Biggs, Mrs. Biggs would have vaporized her.

Instead, Matilda held up a finger. "Yes," she said with a smile. "Thank you. You are quite right. I had forgotten. I was more than fifteen minutes late." She noted this on the paper. Then she tore off the page, crumpled it up, and threw it in the wastebasket. A few people giggled and looked at one another.

"I believe," said Julie, "that you're supposed to take it down to the office."

"I am? Why?"

Everyone shrugged. They had no idea why it mattered to anyone who was or wasn't late or here or not here. So Matilda sighed, bent over the wastebasket, plucked out the wadded-up ball, and started out the door.

"Wait!" cried Raggie. He was a skinny child, small for his age, and with a head of hair that looked as if it had never made the acquaintance of comb or brush. "You're supposed to give it to me. I'm the class monitor this week"—a complete lie, it was actually Simon's turn—"it's my job to take the attendance sheet down."

"And who might you be?"

"I'm Raggie."

"Well, thank you very much, Raggie," said Matilda, handing the crumpled sheet to him. Raggie looked at the ball of paper. Simon knew he was wondering if she really wanted him to take it to the office like that. But Matilda said nothing, so he shrugged and left the classroom.

Sebastian nudged Simon. "What do you want to bet he doesn't come back until recess?" Simon nodded. Raggie used any excuse he could find to get out of the classroom. Once he'd delivered the attendance, most likely he would spend the morning in the library or the bathroom. One time he'd even been caught in the empty science lab making rockets. The last substitute teacher hadn't noticed that Raggie never came back at all.

"Now," said Matilda, rubbing her hands together. "I would like some explanation of this behavior. Why was no one late but me?"

The students all looked at one another. Julie silently

14

mouthed the word *duh* to Simon. Simon ignored her. He slid a bit lower in his seat until only his eyes were showing.

"I *think* that's because we get warnings if we're late," Julie explained slowly and carefully.

"Come, come. Surely they don't punish you for a thing like being a tad late. 'Punctuality is the bugbear of small minds.' It's well known. Or is it 'Consistency is the bugbear of small minds'? Oh dear, I no longer remember."

"And if you get two warnings," continued Julie, "you get a detention." Seeing Matilda's blank look, she explained further. "Detention. You have to stay after school. If you get five detentions, you're suspended for a day."

"Well, well, well," said Matilda. "I always say, if you live long enough, you see everything." She shook her head. "From now on, things are going to be different. I have no problem with people being late. In fact I always try to be a little late myself. It makes things more interesting.

"For example, I was late getting here today because on my way I saw a poor dead porcupine by the side of the road. Now I find dead porcupines fascinating. Well, live ones are even better, aren't they, but beggars can't be choosers and besides it's *so* difficult to get really close to a live porcupine. They seem to mind if you poke your face right into theirs and ask to borrow a few quills. So this was an opportunity not to be missed. I borrowed a few of his quills—he won't need them anymore, poor thing—and then gave him a proper burial."

15

She went over to her purse—it was more like a small suitcase, actually—and pulled out a plastic sandwich bag filled with black-and-white quills. Twenty-four quills, to be precise.

"Cool!" said Ethan.

"Now," said Matilda, "that's what I did while I was being late. What did *you* do while I was being late?"

Simon stared at the ceiling. The other students looked at each other uncertainly and said nothing. Matilda picked up one of Raggie's paper rocket ships, looked at it with interest, and placed it on her desk.

"In the future," she said, "I expect more of you to be late. All you need is a perfectly good excuse, like a dead porcupine. And if I am late, I hope you will have something to show for it. Is that understood?"

The children all looked at one another and nodded dumbly.

"Something like this very fine space vehicle," she continued, "which belongs to whom?"

"It's Raggie's," said Bix.

"And speaking of Raggie," said Matilda, "where the devil has he gotten to?"

The Usual Tricks

Raggie returned much sooner than anyone expected. In fact, he was propelled back into the classroom by the school secretary, Miss Boynton, who had a firm grip on his elbow and a businesslike glint in her eye. Simon knew Miss B was not an unkind person, but she was perpetually overworked and harassed by children who had forgotten their lunches or imagined they were sick or got themselves hit by snowballs at recess, and by parents who could never remember which day was early release day or neglected to send in the proper field-trip forms or resolutely forgot to pay for their children's school lunches. Not to mention principals who never finished their sentences.

She opened the door, surveyed the class, and gave Matilda Maxwell a pitying look.

"He's up to his usual tricks," she said, pushing Raggie through the door. "He had the nerve to pretend *this* was the attendance sheet." She held out a much crinkled sheet of paper.

Mrs. Maxwell took the sheet from Miss Boynton and read aloud, " 'Ethan is a jerk. He has scummy teeth.' "

The class tittered. Bix jabbed Jimmy in the ribs and covered his mouth with his hands. Ethan glared at both of them.

"My, that doesn't sound like the attendance report."

"And he handed it to me all crumpled up in a ball," added the secretary. "I've given him a warning."

"Just a minute," said Matilda. "I think I know what happened."

She fished around in the trash can, which was full of wadded-up "basketballs" from Bix's game that morning. She pulled out another crumpled sheet of paper, unfolded it, and handed it to Miss Boynton. "There, I

18

gave him the wrong sheet. That's the right one. It's entirely my fault. I think there was some confusion over wastebaskets and waste-basket-balls this morning. This note"—she held up the sheet from Miss Boynton—"must belong to someone else in the class." She gazed slowly around the room and then dropped the sheet on Bix's desk. "It must belong to our basketball star. And you would be . . . ?"

"Bix." He was struggling not to laugh.

"Well, Bix, would you mind opening your mouth?"

Bix looked baffled but did as he was told. Matilda peered inside. She turned to Ethan.

"I suppose you are Ethan with the scummy teeth?" Ethan nodded. "Well, you'll be pleased to know that Bix has scummy teeth, too. I would like both of you to spend more time brushing. And it wouldn't kill you to floss, young man." This last comment was directed at Bix, who had buried his head in his arms.

"Excuse me," said Miss Boynton. She was frozen in the doorway, covered with confusion, reading the new attendance report. "This just says, 'Everyone's here. No one's not here. I was late.'"

"That's correct," said Matilda crisply. "I was late. I get a warning."

"But—"

"And Raggie doesn't. Fair's fair. Now off you go." And she hurried the harassed young woman out the door. "We have important work to do."

Funny

Matilda looked around at the class. "I suppose we better start by learning one another's names. My name is Matilda Maxwell, but everyone calls me Mattie. Except you. I'm very old, seventy-four years old, so you will have to call me Mrs. Maxwell. Unless of course"—the tiniest pause—"unless you happen to be my great-nephew or -niece, in which case you may call me Aunt Mattie." Here Simon gave a guilty start, but Aunt Mattie continued as if she hadn't noticed a thing. "I have three llamas, that's spelled with two *l*s, and goodness knows how many cats, and some peacocks, and two horses. Oh, yes, and a husband, too. His name is Mr. Maxwell."

Julie looked at Simon and once again mouthed *duh* at him. Simon gave her a weak smile. He was wondering what the chances were of someone he knew dying in the next ten minutes and his being called to the office and excused from school. For the rest of his life.

Aunt Mattie walked over to the front row. "Now let's start here. What's your name?" she asked a boy in the front row. Simon groaned inwardly. She could hardly have picked a worse person to start with. Simon knew Jimmy would do his best to make things impossible for Aunt Mattie.

Jimmy looked Aunt Mattie straight in the eye.

"My name is Mario," he said. This drew a loud snort from Ethan and several others. Matilda smiled at Jimmy absentmindedly and then asked if she could see his hat. He looked surprised, but removed his baseball cap. She turned it over in her hands curiously.

"The Chicago Bulls," she said. "Is that a meat-packing plant?"

The class burst out laughing. Jimmy rolled his eyes at Ethan. "No," he said. "It's a basketball team. Only the most famous basketball team in the world."

"I see," said Matilda. "And this, then, must be a basketball hat?"

More laughter. Simon wished fervently for a lightning bolt to strike him dead.

"No," said Jimmy. "It's a *baseball* hat."

"I see," said Matilda. "A baseball uniform with the name of a basketball team on it. Very peculiar. But, Mario, do I look like a baseball coach?" The class laughed, and she gestured to the other students. "Does this look like a baseball game?" Several students laughed, and Bix said, "She got you there, Jimmy." Jimmy shrugged, and Matilda went and hung his cap from a coat peg. "From now on, *Jimmy*," she said, with emphasis on *Jimmy*, "I don't expect students to wear baseball caps in class, except, of course, for those times when we are actually playing baseball. Also, I expect them to remember their names. Now then, do you have brothers or sisters?"

"No," said Jimmy, glowering.

"Yes, you do," said Bix, looking surprised. He turned to Matilda. "His brother is this really, really big deal on the high school basketball team. He's going to Duke on a scholarship. And his sister, Emily, she won a national piano contest or something."

"How very exciting," said Matilda. "And do you play sports, or an instrument?"

"Yeah," said Jimmy, shooting Bix a dirty look. "I'm training for the Junior Olympics. As a skeet shooter."

Matilda nodded seriously but said nothing. She then continued around the class. Mandy volunteered that she had one brother and three guinea pigs. Raggie explained that his real name was Frank but he was called Raggie.

"Don't tell me," interrupted Mrs. Maxwell. "You are called Raggie because you have the misfortune to have an older sister who couldn't pronounce your name correctly when you were born."

"Yeah," said Raggie. "How'd you know that?" Simon wished he could tell him that sometimes there were things that Aunt Mattie just *knew*. Once he had been convinced she was a witch.

"Just a good guess. It's a terrible thing to have an older sister."

Raggie nodded. "You aren't kidding," he said. "I have six of them."

When it came to Julie's turn, Simon winced. With

Julie you could never tell what would happen. Jimmy was a menace and a bully, determined to create trouble where, when—and to whom—he could. But at least he was predictable. Julie simply enjoyed being the center of attention. She usually managed to do this by making fun of the grown-ups around her—all grown-ups were fair game, it was nothing personal. (Julie was the one who had invented the game of Sink the Sub.) She had a knack for telling uncomfortable truths, which grown-ups found unnerving. It was equaled only by her talent for telling outrageous lies, which kids found entertaining.

She rose now from her seat with a solemn expression.

"My name is Julie Biedermeyer," she said. "I am the oldest of eight children. My mother"—here she swallowed painfully and looked down at the desk for a moment—"my mother died last year in a"—her voice choked briefly but she went on—"in a tragic meat-packing accident." She sat down abruptly. Beside her Mandy and Mindy were trying hard to keep a straight face.

Matilda nodded gravely. "And what would be the names and ages of your brothers and sisters?"

"Well," said Julie, caught off guard, "there's baby Joey, he's one. And, uh, the twins, two sets of twins in fact: Hughie and Louie, age two, and Harry and uh Larry, they're three. And Elsie, she's four, and Ralph, he's five, and Susie, she's eight, and uh, Sally's nine."

"Let's see, that makes ten children by my count," said Matilda. "You may not be good at math, but your skills as a thespian are impressive. Most impressive. A nice bit of cabotinage."

"Hunh?" said Julie.

"I think she means," hissed Mindy in her ear, "that you're a good actor."

Matilda circled Julie's desk, looking at her carefully. "My guess would be . . . only child."

"Hey!" cried Julie, looking around. "Someone snitched. Who told her?"

"Oh, she just knows," said Simon under his breath. Julie gave him a questioning glance, but he had sunk so low in his chair, in an effort to become invisible, that he could see nothing.

And then it was Simon's turn. There was no more avoiding it. He would not be suddenly summoned to the office. The earth would not open and swallow him. School would not be called off because of a sudden meteor shower. So he pulled himself up in his seat.

"I'm Simon Maxwell," he said, speaking loudly. "I have no brothers or sisters. I have some goldfish, though. And . . . and a pet cat named Raspberry. Which my great-aunt gave me." He looked Aunt Mattie in the eye. Now it would happen. Now everyone would discover that this Mrs. Maxwell was his great-aunt. He wondered if anyone had ever actually died of embarrassment. Actually died and been buried and had it on their gravestone: HERE LIES SIMON. DIED OF MORTIFICATION.

But Mattie gave no sign of recognizing him beyond raising her eyebrows.

"Maxwell?" she asked. "Two Maxwells in the same

room. What a funny coincidence. I'll bet we're related somehow."

"Sure," said Simon as he stared down at his desk, his cheeks burning. "That would be really funny."

Traitor

"Funny," said Aunt Mattie, after consulting her little black teacher's book, "it doesn't say anything here about free time or recess." She looked at Julie. "It says here that Monday mornings we do vocabulary." Julie batted her eyes and smiled innocently.

The class let out a collective sigh. Then they began noisily raising their desk lids and pulling out battered workbooks and pencils. Seeing Mattie's confusion, Mollie got up and found the teacher's copy of the workbook on her desk for her. She opened to Lesson 19: Parts of the Body.

"'Define the following ten words,'" Mattie read aloud, "'and use each in a sentence: *pancreas, gall bladder, trachea, kidney, femur, tibia, cranium, spleen, clavicle, appendix.*' Oh my, no. This will never do."

The children, who were already fighting over the dictionaries, for none of them had ever heard of any of the words, stopped and looked at Matilda. She was frowning at the vocabulary book, flipping through the pages. Then she tossed the whole thing into the wastebasket.

"Why'd you do that?" asked Mindy. "We always use this workbook."

"I never saw so many useless words in my life!" said Matilda. "*Pancreas!* Pah! Whoever heard of a pancreas? When would you ever need to use the word *pancreas*? Never! If your pancreas was ailing, you would go to a doctor and say, 'My belly hurts.' And the doctor would say, 'No, that's your pancreas that hurts.' And you would say, 'Thanks so much for clearing that up.' *Pancreas!* Pah!"

And she marched up and down by the blackboard, her eyes fairly snapping. Finally she stopped.

"Take out your pencils," she commanded. "Write this down." She wrote a long string of words on the blackboard:

quisling
pecksniffian
miscreant
muculent
rodomontade
proficuous
persiflage
cabotinage
sabotage
badinage
nefarious
whiffet

"Those," she said, "now *those* are useful words." She pointed to one at random. "How many people know the meaning of *quisling*? How about *proficuous*?" No one raised a hand. "Very good. We'll start with *quisling*. Write down a definition for it. No, don't touch the dictionaries." The students looked blankly at her.

"But we don't know what it means," said Jimmy.

When Matilda turned away he twirled his finger by his head to indicate that Matilda was missing some of her marbles. Ethan snickered.

"Of course you don't. But you should. It's a very good word. So make up a definition that sounds like what you think *quisling* might mean. Make it sound as much like a dictionary definition as you can. Then use it in a sentence. The point is to see how many people you can fool."

Slowly the students got the idea. They sat giggling, scribbling, and staring off into space. While they worked, Matilda got a battered red dictionary out of her carpetbag, looked up the definition of *quisling,* and wrote it on a piece of paper. Then she collected all the students' "definitions."

"Now," she said, "I'm going to read the fake definitions, as well as the real definition, and your job is to guess which is the real definition. The person who gets the most votes for his or her fake definition is the winner."

She proceeded to read out the answers. Some were stupid, but some were pretty good, Simon thought.

" '*Quisling:* noun. A short quiz. Example: The teacher gave the class a vocabulary quisling.' " Six people voted for that one.

" '*Quisling.* From the verb *to quisle,* meaning to *quickly whistle.* Example: "Could you stop that quisling?" yelled his father. "It's driving me crazy!" ' " Four people voted for that one.

Simon won the game with his: " '*Quisling:* noun. A young bird, the offspring of a *quisse.* Example: The mother *quisse* crossed the road, followed by her six little quislings.' " Eleven people voted for that one.

Nobody voted for the real definition: " '*Quisling:* noun. From the Norwegian politician Vidkun Quisling. A traitor. Example: The quisling was executed for betraying his country.' "

The Way We've Always Done It

The bell sounded, startling Aunt Mattie so much that her pencil flew straight up into the air and impaled itself in her hair. The children stuffed their papers into their desks and jumped up, heading for the door.

"What is it? What's happening?" asked Matilda.

The class ignored her and streamed out of the room. Miss Boynton poked her head inside the door.

"Is there a fire?" Matilda asked her. "A nuclear war? Don't panic, children. Everyone under your desks. Stop, look, and listen. I mean, stop, rock, and roll. That is, stop, drop, and—"

Miss Boynton gave her a strange look. "It's recess time," she explained over the hullabaloo. "You can come to the Teachers Room."

"Goodness," said Matilda. "I'm so relieved. But don't I get to go outside, too?"

Miss Boynton laughed. "No. Lucky you, you don't have recess duty this week. You can come and meet the other teachers. Who's the class monitor? Simon, would you please show Mrs. Maxwell to the Teachers Room?" And before Simon could object, she was gone.

Fortunately, the walk to the Teachers Room was short, and the corridor was so full of noisy kids that speech was impossible. Simon guided Matilda to the nurse's office and pointed to a small room, full of teachers, that opened off it.

"This is it, Aunt—I mean, Mrs. Maxwell," he said, blushing a bright red.

Aunt Mattie looked at him with an absentminded smile. "Yes," she said kindly. "Yes, you'd better call me Mrs. Maxwell when we're in school, don't you think? Thank you, dear." And she entered the room.

Simon, though he knew it was bad manners to eavesdrop, was frozen outside the door in fascination, the kind of fascination that makes you watch terrible things, like car accidents or scary movies, even though you don't want to. He simply couldn't imagine Aunt Matilda in the Teachers Room. He lingered outside the door, pretending to get a drink of water.

Matilda surveyed the Teachers Room and spoke brightly.

"Good morning, everyone. I'm Mrs. Maxwell. I've taken Mrs. Biggs's class for the rest of the year."

There was a pause in the conversation. The teachers looked up at Mattie, some of them shaking their heads and making small clucking sounds of sympathy.

"You poor dear," said Miss Frescobaldi, a small, red-headed woman who taught one of the other fifth grades. She patted Matilda on the arm. "Lucky for you there's only five more weeks of school. Hang in there, and if you need help, I'm just next door. Pound on the wall and I'll be there. That's what poor old Croker used to do. How many did you send to the principal this morning?"

"Why, just Raggie, I suppose," said a surprised Matilda. "Was I supposed to send more? It seemed to me that one person was more than enough to carry the attendance sheet."

The group laughed as if Matilda had made a fine joke.

"No, dear, we mean for disciplinary purposes. When they *misbehave*," explained Miss Frescobaldi.

"But how does that discipline them?"

"It doesn't," said Mr. Farley, the other fifth-grade teacher. Charley Farley. He had sleek dark hair and reminded Simon of a seal. "But it makes them the principal's problem, not yours."

"What does he do to them?"

"He makes them sit in a chair in the hallway."

"And if they're really bad," said someone Simon couldn't see, "he sends them home."

"Which makes them the parents' problem, not the principal's?" guessed Mattie.

"Right!"

Mattie appeared to ponder this for a moment. "Let me see if I have this straight. If a child is refusing to do her multiplication tables, she is excused from math and gets to sit in a chair instead, which must be ever so much nicer than doing math. And if a child is miserable at school and refuses to behave he is given a day off and sent home to play. I'm sure there is logic in there somewhere, but I'm blessed if I can see it."

Simon covered his mouth to smother a laugh. He could see the teachers smiling and looking at one another nervously.

"Ha, ha," said one. "Now you put it like that, it seems a little odd. But it's the way we've always done it." The rest of them nodded.

There was a brief silence. Then Mr. Farley spoke up.

"How is your project coming for the County Science Fair?"

"Science Fair? Oh my. What is that?"

"Every fifth-grade class has to submit a science project," said Mr. Farley. He had a knowing expression on his face. "It's quite a big deal. The winning entry gets a lot of prizes for the school and goes on to the State Science Fair."

"Yeah, listen to him talk," said Miss Frescobaldi. "Farley here has won the County Science Fair the last four years running, and the State Fair twice. What's your secret, Farley? How do you get all the geniuses in your class?"

Mr. Farley looked smug. "Oh, I guess it's just a case of being a good science teacher, a natural talent you might say." Simon nearly laughed out loud again. Right, he thought, a natural talent for cheating.

Mr. Farley looked around at the other two fifth-grade teachers—Aunt Mattie and Miss Frescobaldi. "Besides, it's well known that girls—oh, excuse me, I mean *ladies*—don't understand science." He laughed loudly— a short, barking sound. Just like a seal, thought Simon.

Miss Frescobaldi threw a piece of chalk at Mr. Farley. A sixth-grade teacher snorted in disgust. But Aunt Mattie just smiled. And so did Simon as he walked out to recess. He knew it never paid to underestimate his aunt Matilda.

Fruitcake for Lunch

There was only one topic of conversation at lunch that day: the new sub.

"What a wacko," said Jimmy to Simon, shoveling his limp green beans onto Simon's tray and grabbing Simon's chocolate milk in exchange.

"Trade you this sandwich for your chips, Simon?" said Mario. "Yeah, she must have escaped from the funny farm."

"Well, she definitely came off *some* kind of farm," said Julie, wrinkling her nose and waving her hands in front of it. This got a big laugh from her friends.

"Did you see her *shoes*?" said Mandy. "They don't even match!"

"No kidding," chimed in Mindy. "And that hat! It's like a fruit salad."

"Or Chiquita Banana."

Julie opened a napkin, put it on her head, and put her banana on top of that. She stood up and folded her arms like Chiquita Banana. "I am Chiquita Banana and I'm here to say," she sang in a loud voice that was a perfect imitation of Aunt Mattie's, "how does your *por-porosity gushiate* today?"

Everyone laughed except Raggie and Simon. Raggie just grinned his crooked grin. Simon was wishing for once that no one had sat beside him at lunch. He looked around. It was too late to move to another table.

"I give her a week, max," Julie continued. "I'll bet my best pen. She's out of here in five days." She laid it on the table. It could write in four different colors. "Any takers?" Betting on how long the new teacher lasted was an important part of Sink the Sub. Jimmy put some trading cards on the table.

"Two weeks," he said.

"What?" yelped Julie. "No one's ever lasted more than a week with us. Seven days, max."

Ethan gave a shrug and looked around. "I dunno, Julie," he said. "She could be tough. She's got *you* figured out." He put a yo-yo on the table. "I'm with Jimmy. Two weeks."

"Are you nuts?" cried Julie. "She's a fruitcake! And we're the worst class in the school." Julie's followers looked at Julie. Jimmy's followers looked at Jimmy. Mindy put her new eraser on the table. "I know she's a fruitcake," she said, "but Ethan's right. Two weeks. Sorry, Julie." And one by one everyone else followed suit.

"What about you, Simon?" asked Julie suddenly. "You're being real quiet. Wait a minute—don't tell me you *like* that freak!"

"Omigod, he's gonna be Mrs. Maxwell's little goody-goody," said Jimmy with a sneer. "Just like with Mrs. Biggs. I should've known it wouldn't last."

Simon felt desperate. All eyes were on him. Aunt Mattie just happened to be his favorite relative in the world. Why couldn't he acknowledge her, just tell everyone she was his great-aunt and tell them to shut up about it? What was it about seeing her in front of all his classmates that was so embarrassing? Why was he having to choose between his aunt and his newfound friends?

"She's not so bad," said Simon at last. "She kept Raggie from getting a warning."

A groan of disgust went around the table. Jimmy picked up his tray and moved to a different seat. Before he left, he grabbed Simon's brownie and stuffed it into his ravioli. "Teacher's pet," he hissed.

Simon took a deep breath—he was going to say more, he was going to tell them she was his great-aunt and tell them to shut up about it, he was—but just then Sebastian delivered a sharp kick to his shins. Simon saw that everyone sitting opposite him was looking frozen. He turned around to see what they were all staring at.

Aunt Mattie, lunch bag in hand, was standing right behind him. How long had she been there? How much had she heard? "Is there room for one more?" she asked cheerfully. There was a shocked silence.

"Teachers," said Julie in her direct way, "always eat in the Teachers Room. Unless they have cafeteria duty."

"Oh my," said Aunt Mattie. "So many rules." And she sat down anyway, in the spot Jimmy had vacated. She unrolled the top of her lunch bag, oblivious to the silence at the table, oblivious also to the bread roll, launched from a different table, that hit Moses on the forehead and landed in his ravioli. Moses picked it up and munched it absentmindedly.

"You want to have lunch with *us*?" asked Mario.

"Yes," said Matilda primly. "The Teachers Room is so dreary. And they don't have chocolate milk." She pulled an enormous slab of cake out of her lunch bag. "Questions?"

Silence.

"No questions? Didn't anyone ever teach you to ask questions?"

"Not at school," said Mindy.

"Well, then why are you at school?"

"To learn stuff, I guess."

"And how do you imagine you learn stuff without asking questions?"

38

"You write down what the teacher says. *She's* the one who asks the questions. Like on tests," offered Julie in a slow, I'm-speaking-to-an-idiot-here voice. "We get to *answer* the questions."

"Well, I was always told that the only way to learn something was by *asking* questions," said Aunt Mattie, munching on cake. "And people who don't ask questions are very boring. Like furniture—right, Simon? Furniture doesn't ask questions, and it's dreadfully boring to have around. (My goodness, do you always eat ravioli on your brownie?) So I say again: Questions?"

Julie got that smirk on her face that always preceded some wisecrack.

"Okay," she said, putting down her sandwich. "Why is the sky blue?"

"I don't know," said Matilda. "Because it is. Next question?"

"How many stars are there in the sky?"

"Exactly enough. Enough to read by in some parts of the world. Enough to make you feel really small and unimportant. Next?"

"Have you ever taught before?"

"For one year. When I was twenty."

"Aren't you too old to be a teacher now?"

Matilda, having finished the cake, took a large cucumber sandwich from her bag and began eating that.

"Sometimes," she said, "doing things backward seems to make so much more sense."

"Yeah," muttered Sebastian to Simon, "like eating your dessert first."

"For example, some people take up teaching and

then retire. Like Mrs. Biggs. I retired and then took up teaching.

"Perhaps a better question would have been: Wasn't I too young to teach when I was twenty? Why, when I was twenty, what did I know? Precious little, I can promise you that. Did I know how to change the spark plugs on a V-8 engine? I did not. Did I know what peacock eggs taste like? What a mackerel sky or a red sunset means? How to remove porcupine quills from a dog's nose? That people blink their eyes when they're lying or nervous? How many stars there are in the sky?" She shook her head sadly.

"You still don't know that," Mario pointed out.

"Yes, but I know now that it doesn't matter. In fact, I never want to know exactly how many stars there are. Some things it's best to leave undiscovered. It inspires the imagination. More questions?"

"Why do you wear different shoes?"

Aunt Mattie looked at her feet, as if seeing them for the first time. "Because don't you just love new shoes?" she said. "And hate them, too—they make your feet hurt so. Having two feet hurting all day is a misery, so I break in new shoes one at a time."

"And tomorrow you'll wear the other two?"

"That's right."

Julie rolled her eyes. Everyone else snickered. Simon looked long and hard at his ravioli. He counted them. Thirteen. He had thirteen raviolis. Would lunch never end? Would this day never end?

Stop That Quisling!

Julie lived near Simon's street, and just recently (on those days when Simon didn't take the bus) she had taken to walking home with him. She hadn't asked him. She'd just appeared, sometimes bringing a crowd of giggling girls with her. Simon, who was shy in big groups, pretended to find this tiresome and often ignored them. Secretly, though, he had to admit he found the attention somewhat interesting and even a bit flattering. Today, however, Julie was by herself. Being Julie, she didn't say Hello, or Hey, or any kind of introductory remarks. She just said, "I can't be*lieve* you like that nutcase."

"Well," said Simon, "I—"

"She's a real space cadet, that's what she is. Boy, those shoes! And what about the way she . . ."

Simon slowly tuned out what Julie was saying. One thing about Julie was that she loved the sound of her own voice. Usually this got on Simon's nerves, but today he discovered that it had its good side. It meant he didn't have to do any talking. In a funny way it was kind of peaceful. He could think about whatever he liked, if only he remembered from time to time to say Yeah, or Really? to make it seem like he was listening. And right now he needed to think about what to do about Aunt Mattie.

Aunt Mattie. In a weird way, what had just happened to him was funny. (His dad would have used the word *ironic*.) Simon liked to think that he had had some small part in ridding the school of Mrs. Biggs. That day two months ago, when he had talked back to her for the first time, something in Mrs. Biggs had seemed to snap. She got crabbier and crabbier. And now this—early retirement. Yet Simon also knew that all this change—the change in him, the change in the attitude of the other kids, perhaps even the disappearance of Mrs. Biggs— was due in some strange way to Aunt Mattie, to the two weeks he had spent on her farm.

So Mattie had gotten rid of Mrs. Biggs and helped him make his first friends. And now here she was taking Mrs. Biggs's place and threatening to destroy his budding friendships. Talk about irony!

Okay, the solution was easy. He would just tell everyone she was his great-aunt. What was so hard about that? Well, for one thing, Simon answered his own question, it's way too late. What am I supposed to do, say, Oh, I've just remembered, she's my great-aunt? That would be twice as embarrassing.

"What would?" asked Julie.

"Huh?"

Julie looked pained. "You're talking to yourself. You haven't heard a word I've been saying, have you?"

"Not really." He paused, then turned to Julie. "Can I

ask you a question? Do you ever notice that stuff that seems okay at home seems really dumb at school?"

"What do you mean? Like the food your mother makes? Your lunches and stuff?"

"Yeah. Exactly."

"Tomato sandwiches seem completely normal at home, in fact they taste really good. But when you bring them to school, everybody is like, Gross! And you look at them and they suddenly *do* seem gross. But you never noticed it when your mother makes them for you at home. Stuff like that?"

"That's just what I mean," said Simon, amazed that anyone else might know about this.

"Sure," said Julie. "It's well known. It's the Parallel Universe Phenomenon. School and home exist in two parallel, never-overlapping universes. If by chance they do overlap, disaster."

It made sense. Two separate and distinct universes in a kid's life: There was home, and then there was school. Things that are normal at home are hideous at school. Take his mother's winter coat, for example, or her shoes. Simon hardly noticed and rarely cared what his mother wore around the house. When she showed up at school, however, on those blessedly few occasions, he became painfully aware that her shoes were old-fashioned, that her winter coat was frumpy—no, *ridiculous* was not too strong a word for it. His father, who was a nice enough guy at home, became Super Nerd when he walked through the school door. Why did he wear those really stupid cardigan sweaters? Good grief—*nobody* wore button-up sweaters! Nobody but Mr. Rogers from the kiddie TV show. Did his dad live in a different time zone? A different universe? Yes, a different universe. That was the answer.

And so it had been with Aunt Mattie. That hat! That dress! When he'd been on Mattie's farm, sure they looked a little different, but different had seemed fine, even wonderful. But that was home. This was school. Under the fluorescent glare of the school lights and the disbelieving stares of the other students, Aunt Mattie suddenly seemed like something from a circus.

"So when, say, your parents come to school, do you wish they wouldn't?"

"Of course," said Julie.

"You don't think that's like . . . betraying them?"

"No way! I mean, why should I have to suffer just because my mother decides to drive the world's dorkiest car? Or because my father wears rubbers over his shoes?"

Simon couldn't believe someone else knew about these things. Julie was smart. You could tell by the way she understood stuff that no one else did. She might even understand about Aunt Mattie. He turned to her.

"Julie—" he began, but Julie was still talking, and you might as well try to stop a freight train as stop Julie when she was still talking.

"Sometimes," she was saying, "sometimes I pretend I don't know them. Sometimes I even wish my parents had a different last name so no one would know we are related, you know what I mean?"

"Yeah," said Simon. "It's funny you said that because—" But Julie was still talking.

"Hey, and speaking of having the same last names, you and Mrs. Maxwell—"

This time it was Julie who was interrupted as Mindy, Mandy, and Sebastian overtook them on the sidewalk. "Still talking about the sub?" Sebastian asked Julie. They ignored Simon.

Instead of answering, Julie pulled off her glasses and put them on top of her head, as Aunt Mattie frequently did. "Goodness me," said Julie in her best Aunt Mattie voice, groping blindly around. "Where are my blessed glasses? Who are you? Where am I?"

Sebastian laughed. He, Mindy, and Mandy walked off with Julie, giggling loudly as they went. Simon watched them go. Julie had apparently forgotten he was in the middle of talking to her.

"Look!" cried Mindy. She wore her hair in a ponytail, and this allowed her to take two pencils and stick them into her hair, exactly as Aunt Mattie had stuck pencils into the hair she wore at the back of her head in a loose bun. "I know I have a pencil somewhere," said Mindy, looking vaguely around. This brought fresh gales of laughter from everyone. Simon couldn't stand it anymore.

"Stop!" he said. Everyone turned to stare at him.

"Stop what?" said Julie.

Simon hesitated, feeling all eyes on him. "Stop, rock, and roll!" It was his best imitation of Aunt Mattie's voice. "Don't panic, children. Is it a nuclear war?"

Sebastian laughed. Julie laughed. The whole group laughed. Simon laughed until his sides hurt.

No, she was no relative of his. The names? Just a coincidence. There were plenty of Maxwells in the world. Betrayal? Simon would have denied her three— no, thirty—more times before the day was done.

Please and Thank You

The bell rang at precisely twenty-three minutes past eight the next morning. Simon was already at his desk. Students poured into the classroom, shouting and jostling each other. At precisely twenty-seven minutes past eight, Aunt Mattie appeared in the doorway, completely out of breath and with her hair in wild disarray. In one hand she carried her suitcase of a purse, in the other a large covered cage. Simon recognized that cage, and he smiled in spite of himself.

Aunt Mattie glanced up at the clock.

"Oh dear. Only four minutes late. I must remember to wear my watch tomorrow, so I can be a little less punctual."

She placed the cage in the well under her desk, removed her coat, and began trying—with absolutely no success at all—to pin her hair back up on top of her head.

"Well, and how does your corporosity seem to gashiate this morning, children?" she puffed. She looked about the room expectantly, but again nobody seemed to have the foggiest idea how to answer this question. Simon alone knew that the correct response was "very discombobulate, great congruity, dissimilarity" (whatever that meant). But he bowed his head and kept silent.

Aunt Mattie beamed at the class nonetheless. "Let's see," she said. "If I'm correct, the first thing to do today is to take attendance. Everyone who's here, raise your hands, please. Hmm. Everyone's here. Now everyone who's not here, please raise your hands. Hmmph. It would appear that no one's *not* here." She noted this down and then glared around the room. "Did I not tell you quite clearly yesterday that I expect you to be a little late at least some of the time? Well? Yes, Julie."

"Excuse me, Mrs. Maxwell, ma'am," she said, standing up with a fake-serious expression on her round face. "But Bix isn't here." She pointed to his empty seat and sat down with a sly smile.

"Well," said Matilda crisply, "why didn't he raise his hand then? Hmm?" She bent over her desk and noted Bix's absence on a piece of paper. While doing this, and without raising her eyes from the desk, she said, "And Simon, would you like to share that note with the whole class, please."

Simon, caught dead in the act of passing a note from Julie to Mindy, glanced at the piece of paper, saw what Julie had written about Aunt Mattie, and blushed deep red. "I, um—" he stammered. Simon's cheeks were so hot he thought they might actually burst into flame. Julie, seeing that he was about to read the note, shot him a dirty look and snatched the paper from his hand. She glanced at the note.

48

"It says, 'I think Mrs. Maxwell is the most excellent teacher in the whole world, don't you agree?'" And before anyone could move, she crumpled up the note into a little ball, put it in her mouth, chewed twice, and swallowed it. Mrs. Maxwell waited for the laughter to die down.

"Thank you, my dear," she said. "Well, I've heard of people having to *eat their words* before, but this is the first time I've actually seen it done in public."

The class laughed again, even louder, and Simon breathed a sigh of relief. He would have to say that that round went to Aunt Mattie (and Julie, looking sulky, clearly knew it). But he was mainly relieved to have been saved from reading the note aloud.

"Now then, class," began Aunt Mattie, "where were we? Oh, yes. Attendance. Well, we've finished with that." She tossed the sheet aside. "Let's get down to the business of learning something. Today we do science." She marched to the front of the class. "In science today we are going to study the feather and the quill—"

At that moment, the teacher's desk, which had never been known to speak before, said:

"Shut up!"

The students sat in stunned silence. Not only had the desk spoken for the first time in memory, but it had used a loud, raspy, and disrespectful voice. A voice that Simon knew only too well.

"Oh dear," said Aunt Mattie, bending down and peering under her desk. "Now, Runcible, if you wish to come to school, I expect you to set a better example for the children. At the very least, you must learn to say *please:* 'Shut up, *please.*' Do you hear me?"

She pulled the large cage out from its hiding spot, placed it on the desk, and removed the cover. Inside was a big gray parrot, preening her feathers in a way that could only be described as self-satisfied. She gave Mattie a steely look.

"Say please," said the parrot, cocking her head. "Say thank you." And then, in rapid fire like a machine gun, "Pleasethankyoupleasepleasethankyoupleasethankyouthank—"

"Oh, do shut up!" said Mattie irritably, placing the cover back on her cage.

"Say please!" added Runcible in a muffled voice.

"Please," said Matilda meekly, looking embarrassed. "She always has to have the last word. Such a badly behaved creature."

At this point the class could no longer contain its glee.

"It's a parrot!" they shouted.

"No, it's not," said Matilda. "It's a science experiment." And she removed a feather from the bottom of Runcible's cage and put the cage back under her desk. "A very badly behaved science experiment. As I was saying, the quill—"

Matilda was startled by a loud bell a few feet from her desk. The feather flew into the air. Matilda gave the bell a fierce look and waited impatiently for it to finish jangling.

"Not a nuclear war?" she asked the class.

"No," said Julie. "Just the first bell."

Matilda retrieved the feather and continued: "As I was saying, we are going to study the feather and the quill." From one of the many pockets in her apron she produced the porcupine quills. From another she produced a giant magnifying glass.

"The quill—" Here she was interrupted yet again, this time by Mandy.

"Is this for Science Fair?" she asked. "Because—"

"No," said Matilda tartly. "This is because I found a porcupine yesterday. Now then, the quill—" Overhead, the PA system gave off a loud crackle.

"Good morning, children," came a raspy voice from

the PA, sounding remarkably like Runcible. "Time for morning announcements." The voice began to drone on and on. Morning announcements appeared to be the signal for everyone in the class to start talking at once. Sebastian elbowed Simon. Mandy passed a note to Mindy. Jimmy tried to pull another boy's chair out from under him. And Raggie and Julie announced that they needed to go to the bathroom—*please,* said Julie, she couldn't hold it any longer *please* could she have a bathroom pass please please *please.*

Mrs. Maxwell simply stood at the front of the class, still holding the quill, feather, and magnifying glass, but with an expression on her face that did not bode well. Simon knew that look. It was the look that Uncle Philbert, Aunt Mattie's husband, often got when he was about to let someone have it. But he'd seen it on Aunt Mattie's face only once, when she chewed out a young policeman for speeding.

Gradually the class settled down. Julie decided that she really could hold it. Raggie, nailed by a look from Aunt Mattie, stopped trying to sneak out the door. And Sebastian told Simon to shut up *please.*

Matilda drew a long breath and began a fifth time. "The quill—"

This time the door opened, and the assistant principal stuck his head in the room.

"Attendance sheet!" he announced importantly. "We don't have your attendance sheet, Mrs. Maxwell."

Aunt Mattie turned to face him.

Simon closed his eyes and prayed for a miracle. This was not going to be pretty.

52

5-3, Aunt Mattie

The assistant principal's name—to the delight of the students—was Otis Lister. Mister Lister. He had a long, thin face and long, thin hair combed back over his balding head. His eyes bulged slightly, which Simon thought made him look like a fish, and his face wore a perpetually pinched and put-upon look. It was the look of someone who had spent his entire childhood putting up with a great deal of teasing about his first name. It was the look of someone who had spent his entire adult life putting up with a great deal of impertinence about his last name. It was the look of an assistant principal who spent most of his day dealing with paperwork. An assistant principal who thought he should have been made head principal long, long ago.

"Your attendance sheet is late," repeated Mr. Lister. "I hope—"

"Mr. Lister," interrupted Aunt Mattie tartly, "did no one ever teach you it is bad manners to interrupt?"

Mr. Lister's face went blank.

"I beg your—"

"Interrupting! It's very rude. And was that you on the public address system this morning?"

"Well, yes, I always—"

"So that makes twice you have interrupted my class. And the bell makes three."

That was not entirely fair, as it wasn't Mr. Lister's fault that the bells went off when they did. Nonetheless, Simon began to enjoy this. He knew from personal experience that Aunt Mattie was a champion interrupter herself. Why, if there had been an Olympic event in Interruption, she would have been the odds-on favorite for a gold medal. Mr. Lister may have interrupted her twice this morning, but by Simon's count Aunt Mattie had already interrupted Mr. Lister three times in less than thirty seconds. It was going to be a good contest.

Simon's class, reputed to be the noisiest one in the entire history of the whole elementary school, was utterly silent. You could, thought Simon, have heard a fly sneeze.

Mr. Lister seemed frozen in time and space. Aunt Mattie, on the other hand, marched over to her desk, shuffled through an enormous heap of loose papers, found the attendance sheet at last, handed it to him, and turned back to her students.

"Now class," she began again, "the quill—"

But Mr. Lister was not going to go down in defeat quietly. He looked at the attendance sheet. Would he attempt another interruption, Simon wondered? Yes! He opened his mouth—he was going for it!

"This just says—" began Mr. Lister.

"I've given you fair warning, Mr. Lister," said Aunt

Mattie. "Which you chose to ignore. Now I'm going to have to give you a real warning." She made a note on a scrap of pink paper and then marched over to the door.

"But—"

"And if you persist," said Aunt Mattie, trying gently but firmly to close the door on him, "I'll have to send you to the principal's office. Good day, Mr. Lister."

"But—"

"Shut up!" squawked a voice from the teacher's desk. Mr. Lister poked his head back through the door. His eyes darted around the classroom in disbelief. His mouth opened and closed noiselessly, like one of Simon's goldfish. Then Aunt Mattie closed the door on him with a click. "Good riddance," the desk called out after him. And then, as if remembering a distant lesson, it added in a sulky tone, "Please."

"Really, Runcible, do you *always* have to have the last word?" asked Aunt Mattie.

"Go, Runcible!" shouted Sebastian, and everyone cheered.

"Thank you," said Runcible.

Simon added up the score on his fingers: 5–3, a clear victory for Aunt Mattie. And not just over Mr. Lister, either, he thought, looking around the class.

A Change of Plans

Aunt Mattie stood at the front of the class. She opened her mouth.

"Now, children," she began, "the quill—" But once again, before she could get any further, the bell went off. Matilda closed her mouth grimly.

"I forbid you to move," she said to the students. When the bell had finished its ringing, she placed the quill and magnifying glass back in her bag and rummaged around in it for a moment. Then she straightened up and surveyed the silent classroom.

"I've changed my mind about the science lesson today," she said. "We're not going to study quills." She glanced at the PA loudspeaker and the bell located over the door of the room. "We're going to study electricity." She held up a screwdriver and some pliers. "Does anyone have any wire cutters?"

In Which Mr. Bickle . . .

DETENTION:
Otis Lister
DATE:
REASON:
SIGNED BY:

"Rank insubordination!" fumed Mr. Lister, pacing up and down. "That's what it is. Rudeness and insubordination! Why, she threatened to send me to the principal's office! Me! The assistant principal! And then she told me to shut up! She has to go. Now. I insist."

Herbert J. Bickle shifted in his chair. He squared the edges of some papers on his desk. He cleared his throat. "I see. Yes. Clearly she has behaved in a fashion that is most, and that we . . . understand your . . . However, the fact remains that we cannot, we simply *cannot* afford . . . Otis, you have no idea how many substitutes we called before we found Mrs., uh . . . But at such short notice we couldn't, we just . . . and furthermore the class has a reputation for devouring substitute teachers, quite shocking and, that is to say, and those few people who *could* come at short notice didn't *want* to tackle such a challenging group of, of—"

"Of smart alecks and dunces," said the exasperated Mr. Lister, finishing at least one sentence for Mr. Bickle.

"Well, I would not choose . . . Those exact words are

not how I myself would describe . . . Granted they are a challenging—"

"So we're stuck with this Maxwell woman, is that what you're telling me?"

"In a word, um."

Mr. Lister turned away to hide his irritation. Then he had a sudden inspiration. "Why don't you let me take over the class? I could whip those kids into shape in no time."

Mr. Bickle looked astonished. "You? Take over the . . . ? But I thought you hated the kids in that . . . and teaching is not your, not your best . . ."

"I'm a great teacher," said Mr. Lister. "The students all love me. They do. Children always appreciate firmness and discipline."

"Otis. It won't, it's not . . . I hate to disappoint . . ."

But Mr. Lister stormed out before Mr. Bickle could finish not finishing his sentences, leaving Mr. Bickle staring at the empty space in front of his desk where Otis Lister had so recently been.

For Richard Stands

"There," said Aunt Mattie with a sigh. "Perhaps now we'll have some peace and quiet."

Simon climbed down off the chair, and the class stared at the disassembled PA system and bell. Wires stuck out of the wall in every direction. Several students giggled.

His great-aunt walked to the blackboard and began drawing a diagram of wires and batteries, talking as she went.

". . . and so," she concluded, "it is perfectly clear, is it not, how electricity works?" The sound of a bell ringing could be heard in Miss Frescobaldi's classroom next door. "Can anyone explain why our bell is not ringing at this moment? Mollie?"

But Julie stuck her hand up first.

"Yes, Julie? Can you explain to us why the bell is not ringing?"

"Well, I was going to say, are we still doing Science? Because Science goes from 8:43 until 9:15. It's 9:15 now. Time for Social Studies. That goes until 9:48."

Matilda looked amazed. "Do you mean to tell me you

have thirty-two minutes for Science, then you stop whatever you're doing and do Social Studies for thirty-three minutes?"

The class all nodded.

"Why?" asked Aunt Mattie.

"I don't know," said Julie. "That's just the way it's always done."

"Perhaps, " said Matilda, pacing in front of the blackboard, "perhaps they think because you are young whiffets you aren't capable of concentrating for more than thirty-three minutes at a time? Is that it? My dear, it makes no sense. If you had porch steps that needed fixing and a shed that needed painting and a lawn to mow, would you spend thirty-three minutes fixing the steps and then go paint for thirty-three minutes and drop your brushes and go mow the grass for thirty-three minutes? No, you wouldn't. You'd mow the whole lawn and then fix the steps. And then you'd stop and eat cookies and drink some lemonade for a good long time. And tomorrow you'd start painting the shed."

The class giggled. Even Simon allowed himself a smile. Aunt Mattie definitely had a way of making you see things differently.

"Imagine if grown-ups ran *their* lives that way," said Matilda sternly. "What would that be like?"

Moses, a boy who had never stuck his hand up before, raised his hand now. "It would be like if your mother got halfway through the grocery shopping and she left her cart in the middle of the aisle because it's time to go do laundry."

Mollie stuck up her hand. "Or, you'd call the police

60

because a burglar is breaking into your home," she said, giggling. "And the policeman would arrive and look at his watch and he'd be like, 'Sorry, lady, can't stay, I have to go direct traffic now for the next thirty-three minutes.' "

"Or you call the fire department because your house is on fire," offered Mandy, "and they get halfway there and then turn around because it's time for washing the fire truck."

By this time the whole class was laughing. Matilda held up her hands for silence.

"I think you get the picture. In my class, at any rate, we work on something until it's done. Understood? Now then, where were we? Mollie, can you tell me why the bell is not ringing?"

Mollie looked at the diagram, looked at the bell. "Because you broke the circuit?" she said.

"Exactly," said Matilda. The sound next door had changed to the muffled tones of the PA. "Would you like to demonstrate to us how that works?"

Mollie looked uncertain.

"Go ahead," urged Mattie. "Climb right up there."

So Mollie climbed onto the chair, picked up one of the dangling PA wires, peered for a few seconds at the box, looked at the diagram on the blackboard, and stuck the wire into the box. Instantly the voice of Mr. Lister could be heard.

"—please rise for—" Mollie pulled the wire out and then in and out again, with the result that Mr. Lister's voice came across in quick staccato bursts: "—ledge of Alleg . . . the fla . . . United Sta . . . merica—" The class cheered, and Mollie climbed down, made a brief bow to the class, and took her seat. Simon, sitting next to Julie, saw her nudge Mandy in the ribs. Mandy tried to ignore her.

"Very good," said Matilda, returning to her desk. "And now that you all understand electrical circuits, let us move on to the porcupine quill." She pulled the quill from her pocket just as Julie hissed, "Go on!" at Mandy. "The quill—" Mattie began, but stopped when she saw a raised hand. "Yes, Mandy," she said, with just the tiniest hint of irritation.

"We're supposed to do the Pledge of a Legions now," said Mandy, with a look at Julie.

"We *have* to," said Julie.

"Yeah," said Raggie. "Or we'll be arrested or something. For being *quislings*," he added brightly.

"Oh my," said Matilda. "Well, we can't have that. Very well, proceed."

The children rose dutifully, faced a flag in the corner of the room, and placed their hands in what they imagined to be the general area of their hearts.

"I plejuleejunz," droned the class in dull, sing-song voices. They mumbled along to the end and sat down with a clatter of chairs.

Matilda looked at them. "Everyone take out a piece of paper," she commanded. The class stared at her. "A piece of paper and a pencil." The students obeyed, mutely. "Now, would everyone please write down the Pledge of Allegiance."

As Simon worked, Julie nudged him. "It's your turn next," she whispered, without taking her eyes from her work. Simon looked at her blankly. "To interrupt her, stupid." But Simon had had time to think about the way he'd acted yesterday. It was one thing, he decided, to be unable to admit Mrs. Maxwell was his aunt; it was quite another thing to make fun of her and take part in Sink the Sub. He shook his head firmly and concentrated on his paper. Julie gave him a black look and then, while Aunt Mattie wasn't looking, wrote a note and passed it to Sebastian. Sebastian read it. He, too, shook his head.

Minutes later Matilda collected the papers, read

through them, and then faced the class. "Can anyone tell me what the Pledge of Allegiance means?" Silence. "Does anyone know what *allegiance* means?" The students looked at one another and shrugged. Julie glanced around the class and then put up her hand.

"Are we doing Social Studies now?" she asked.

"Yes, we're doing Social Studies," said Matilda tartly. "Whatever that means." She turned and, glancing through the students' papers, began to write on the board. This is what she wrote:

I pledge a legions to the flag of the Untied States of America. Undo the republic, for Richard Stands, one Asian, under God, invisible, with liberty, injustice for all.

"Does anybody have the faintest idea what that means? No? But you stand here day after day, year after year, with your hands firmly on your hearts, or what you imagine to be your hearts because I notice that most of you put your hands on your clavicle or possibly your pancreas, and you make a solemn promise. To protect liberty and 'injustice.' To be loyal to Richard Stands, whoever he might be. A mysterious Asian, it seems. An invisible Asian at that. Land sakes, children. Where do you park your brains when you come to school? Eh? Well, I guess we have our work cut out for us this morning, don't we?"

And that morning no one heard the bell for recess because they were busy figuring out who Richard Stands was.

Or maybe it was because the bell never rang.

Lemon Meringue Pi?

SCHOOL SCIENCE
FAIR left
2 weeks left

After recess, Matilda pulled the quills out of her apron pocket and faced the class. Simon didn't want to be the one to do it, but somebody had to remind her. He stuck his hand up.

"The quill," began Aunt Matilda. She stopped. "Yes, Simon?"

"Excuse me," he said. "But we're supposed to be working on our Science Fair project now. There are only a few weeks left." At this the whole class groaned.

"Why don't you keep your mouth shut, Simon?" said Jimmy under his breath. "Thanks a whole lot."

Matilda looked thoughtful. "Yes, I suppose we should be thinking about the Science Fair. What is your project?"

Mollie trudged over to the corner of the room and picked up a huge scroll of white paper. Mandy helped her unroll it.

"Pi," said Mollie.

"Pie? That sounds fun. What kind of pie?"

"No, not that kind of pie. This kind of pi." Mollie and Mandy unrolled the paper. It spread all the way across the blackboard and was covered with the biggest single long-division problem Matilda had ever seen. The answer to it, so far, was: 3.14159265358979323846264338 32795028841971693993751058209749445923078164 06286208998628034825341.

"Pi," explained Simon, "is how you get the circumference of a circle, or something like that. It's a fraction. No matter how far you divide it out, it keeps on going. On and on forever. No one's ever gotten to the end of it. Mrs. Biggs thought it would be fun to try figuring it out to a hundred places. We had to work on it every day. If we were bad, we worked on it extra."

"Oh my. And is it?"

"What?"

"Fun?"

Another groan was her answer.

"Are you learning anything by doing it?"

"How to die of boredom," said Jimmy. "Which we already knew."

"Yeah, see, Mrs. Biggs loves math. She went to MIT or something."

Aunt Mattie looked at the scroll. Then she went to her desk, opened drawers, and rummaged around for a moment. "What I don't understand," she said at last, "is why you don't just do this." And, producing a large calculator, she punched some numbers in. "There. That's your answer. Or close enough." She rolled up the pi scroll and put it in a closet.

The students looked at her, dumbfounded.

"Now, let's try to think up a more interesting science project. Ideas?"

Simon glanced around the class. No one seemed the least bit interested in the topic. Mario yawned. Sebastian began doodling on his homework assignment sheet. Mollie was whispering to Mindy, who had her head in a book.

"Come, come. Surely there's something we could do."

"What's the point?" said Jimmy. "We'll never win anything. Mr. Farley's class is going to win again. They always do. So why bother?"

"What are they doing?" asked Matilda.

"Nothing much. Just building a computer," said Jimmy. Everyone slumped in their desks at this reminder. "It's way cool. They've been working on it since school started. No way we can beat it."

"A computer? Fifth graders? Goodness me, how ambitious."

"Yeah, well, Wilton Pflummerfield is in that class."

"Who's he? A computer genius?" asked Matilda. The class burst into laughter.

"Let me put it this way," said Julie. "That boy is so dumb, he thinks chocolate milk comes from brown cows."

"You astonish me," said Mattie.

"He acts like he's smart—but he's not," explained Ethan.

"The lights may be burning," continued Julie, "but nobody's home. The TV's on, but it's not plugged in, if you get my drift."

"The monitor's working, but the hard drive ain't," said Mario, getting into the spirit. Simon could see that Julie was on a roll, and she had the rest of the class with her again.

"Yeah," said Mindy. "It's a big fat book, but the pages are all blank."

"His elevator," said Bix, "doesn't go all the way to the top floor."

Mattie stopped them. "I think I get the picture," she said. "He's not the brightest star in the sky, poor child. But how does that help his class with—"

"His dad is *Mr. Pflummerfield*," said Simon, trying to help Aunt Mattie out.

"Of course he is," said Matilda. "Stands to reason that Wilton Pflummerfield's dad would be called Mr. Pflummerfield." Simon sighed.

"Pflummerfield," repeated Julie patiently, as Matilda showed no signs of recognition. "As in Pflummerfield Home Computing. Pflummerfield Electronics & Engineering. The big computer makers? Everybody's heard of them, unless they've been on Mars or someplace."

Aunt Mattie simply shrugged at this, and Simon could practically hear the other students concluding that, yes, she obviously *had* been on Mars or someplace. After all, she thought the Chicago Bulls were a meat-packing plant.

"The point is," she said, "why would anyone *want* to build a computer for the Science Fair? There are far too many computers in the world already. Do we really need another? No, no," she continued, answering her own question, "we must think of something more original. More useful. Something the world does need. Not another computer." She smiled at the class. "We will come up with the most exciting Science Fair project in years, I can feel it."

The class did not appear to share her enthusiasm. There was a glum silence.

"I guess nobody told you," said Mario at last. "We're the stupid class. We're not good at anything. And we're worst at math and science."

"Rubbish," said Mrs. Maxwell. "Everyone's good at something."

"It's not rubbish, Mrs. Maxwell," said Mindy. "We're the only class in the school that has never even won a Math Bee. If we can't win a crummy Math Bee, how can we win the County Science Fair?"

"Well," said Matilda, surveying the gloomy class, "the answer is very clear. We will start by winning the Math Bee." She tossed the calculator back in the drawer and smiled broadly. "Whatever that is."

Oops

It fell to Simon to explain to Aunt Mattie the details of the Math Bee. It was lunchtime, and Simon found himself, once again, sitting alone. (Well, not exactly alone, but to Simon's mind, fifth-grade girls didn't really count.) And then Aunt Mattie came, with her brown lunch bag, and sat herself down at the end of the long table. Today, Simon noticed, she was wearing the other pair of mismatched shoes, and enormously long, dangly earrings. At least the earrings matched.

The Math Bee, Simon explained, in answer to Aunt Mattie's question, had been Mrs. Biggs's idea of a *really* fun time. "She'd get teams from all the fourth or fifth grades or whoever together in the auditorium," he went on. "It's sort of like one of those old TV quiz shows, where they had college teams competing against each other. The whole school watches."

"You'll get to see for yourself," said Mollie with a sigh. "Fifth grades are having one this Friday."

"Five kids from each class sit up on the stage," continued Simon. "Mrs. Biggs fires math problems at them as fast as she can: What's 76 times 54? Or 127 divided by 13? The first kid to get the right answer wins points for the team. Wrong answers cost you points."

"And what do you win?" asked Matilda.

"Usually the team—the class—gets to take a day off from school to go on some field trip or other," said Mandy.

"Well, that could come in handy," mused Matilda, looking around at the students. "Yes, that's a very nice prize for a Math Bee."

The word *prize* must have caught Mr. Farley's ear as he walked by, for he stopped. "The Math Bee prize?" he asked. "You don't imagine *you're* going to win, do you?" The students were already picking up their trays and lunch boxes—they ate in a matter of nano-seconds—and perhaps that's why Mr. Farley didn't bother to lower his voice. But Matilda spoke up, loud enough to cause the students to stop and listen.

"Oh, no," she said. "I don't *imagine* we're going to win."

"Good," said Mr. Farley. "Because—"

"I *know* we're going to win." Charley Farley threw his head back and snorted with amusement. This made him look so much like a seal Simon could hardly stand it. He should be balancing a ball on the end of his nose right now, he thought.

"Can't miss, dearie," continued Aunt Mattie. She gave Simon a conspiratorial wink. "I have a secret weapon."

"Sure you do," said Mr. Farley, still laughing. "You're going to feed your kids toxic waste and turn them into Teenage Mutant Math Champs. Hey, speaking of prizes, have you had a chance to work on that Science Fair project yet? You know, the Giant Pi in the Sky? Now there's a real winner, eh?" He laughed and patted Matilda on the shoulder.

"Oh, we've abandoned the pi project," said Aunt Mattie. "We're starting a new one."

"With only two weeks to go until the fair? What is it?"

"We don't know yet. But it'll be a winner. Won't it, Simon?" She ignored Mr. Farley's snort of disbelief. "And how is your project going?"

"We're going to amaze them this year." He smiled expansively. "I wouldn't be surprised if we went on to win the State—no, the National—Science Fair. Imagine, a working computer!"

"And all done by fifth graders?" asked Aunt Mattie innocently. "All by themselves?"

Mr. Farley just laughed. "Smartest darn fifth graders you ever saw," he said, with a wink at the two of them. "Especially that Pflummerfield boy."

Simon was waiting in line behind Raggie to scrape his uneaten meal into the garbage when Miss Boynton came up to Aunt Mattie as she was leaving the cafeteria.

"How are you doing, dear?" Miss Boynton asked, raising her eyebrows in a way that could only mean: Ready to shoot yourself yet?

"Fine, just fine," said Aunt Mattie. "Quite an engaging group of youngsters."

"Are you aware you've set a school record?"

"Indeed? In what way?"

"Two whole days and not a single child sent to Mr. Bickle's office. A record for a substitute in that class. Have you handed out any warnings? Mrs. Biggs used to hand them out with a shovel—especially to poor Raggie and that Jimmy."

"Why, yes, I've given out quite a few, mostly to myself, though: for being late, forgetting to send attendance sheets in, and so on."

Miss Boynton raised her eyebrows in surprise. "Indeed? Well, if your Raggie gets many more warnings, he's in major trouble. He just got one from Mr. Farley for not having a hall pass."

Simon shot a look at Raggie, but Raggie didn't appear to be listening to the conversation.

"Does that mean he has to stay after school Tuesday?"

"Yes. And one more detention, and he's out of here. Suspended."

"Oh dear," said Aunt Mattie to herself. "I'll have to start passing out more warnings, then." And she hastened out into the hall, leaving Miss Boynton shaking her head in amazement.

At that moment Simon received a shove from the rear. Ethan and Jimmy were behind him with their lunch trays. "Did you have a nice lunch with the teacher?" sneered Jimmy. "I see you're back to being teacher's pet."

"Sucking up, as usual," said Ethan disgustedly. Then, before Simon could reply, they shouldered past him and Raggie, and as they did so, the leftover spaghetti from Jimmy's tray somehow spilled onto Simon and Raggie.

"Oops," snickered Jimmy, and turned his back.

Raggie looked down at his ruined clothes. "I'm dead," he said.

Simon looked at his own neat white shirt, now stained tomato red. And then, before he knew what he was doing, he had upended his tray on Jimmy's head.

Dangerously Slippery

"An accident, you say?"

Jimmy nodded. He appeared a little disconcerted. Maybe it was the bits of spaghetti still clinging to his ear. Or maybe he just wasn't used to talking to someone who was knitting.

"Yeah," he managed to say. "I just like bumped into him and everything spilled. By accident." He shot Simon a defiant look.

"Simon? Is that what happened?" Aunt Mattie glanced up from her knitting, giving Simon a distracted look, and said, "Knit one, purl two."

"He—" It was a simple act, but one that Simon had never done before. He had never lied. Ever. "Yes, he must have slipped."

"And how did *your* tray end up on *his* head? Knit two, purl one, cast off."

"I don't remember, it just sort of—"

"He slipped, too," said Jimmy.

"I see. And you, Raggie? Do you have anything to say?"

Raggie, staring at the floor, just shook his head.

Silence, but for the sound of knitting needles clicking softly.

"Jimmy, how many detentions do you have so far this year?"

"Three."

"Two more and you get suspended?"

"Yeah, so, big whoop."

"Will your parents think it's a big whoop?"

"They don't care," said Jimmy. "They probably won't even notice. They're too busy going to basketball games and piano recitals."

"What about you, Raggie? You have four detentions?"

Raggie nodded. He ducked his chin, pulled the edge of his T-shirt up into his mouth and started chewing on it. His T-shirts were all raggedy from his chewing on them all the time.

"And if you get suspended, what happens? Does your family notice?" There was a long silence while Raggie gnawed his T-shirt. "Knit two, purl two," said Aunt Mattie to her needles. Then Raggie wiped his nose with the back of his wrist.

"My dad," he said in a whisper, "will kill me."

The needles stopped their clicking. Aunt Mattie rummaged around in her suitcase of a purse and produced a small bottle labeled Surefire Llama Spit Stain Remover. "Well, then, I suggest you go clean up. Take this. It not only vaporizes llama spit, but is guaranteed to send spaghetti stains packing as well." Raggie nodded, grabbed the bottle, and vanished. Mattie turned back to Simon and Jimmy.

"In the future, try to watch where you're going,

especially when carrying spaghetti. The floors in this school appear to be dangerously slippery. By the way," she added, "I'm pairing up children in the class to work on the Science Fair project. You three boys will be a team. I want you to move your desks together." Simon and Jimmy looked at each other wordlessly. Finally Aunt Mattie spoke again.

"I'm worried about young Raggie. We must do everything we can to keep him from getting suspended—not just for his sake, but for the whole class's. I have a hunch he may be very helpful with this Science Fair project. I need someone who will look out for him." She looked at Simon, who was about to speak. But before he could open his mouth, her glance slid right past him to Jimmy.

"Jimmy," she said, "I want you to be his guardian angel. Can you do that? Can you keep Raggie out of trouble, keep an eye on our little escape artist? Kind of like a big brother?"

Simon saw the surprise in Jimmy's eyes and felt, with the force of total certainty, that no one had ever asked him to do anything like this before. He saw Jimmy wrestling with the question. He could practically hear him thinking: Hey, this is not cool. And, What about Sink the Sub? And, Who cares about the dumb Science Fair?

And he saw that it surprised Jimmy as much as anyone else when he answered, "I dunno. Maybe. Yeah, I could do that, I guess."

"Good," said Aunt Mattie crisply. "See that you do. Never let him out of your sight. He's a regular Houdini, he is. Why, he's probably halfway to New York right now." Her needles resumed their clicking. Her fingers flew over the wool. "Cast off," she said. And the two boys left, though they couldn't be sure if she was talking to them, or to her knitting.

The Secret Weapon

Aunt Mattie brought the class to attention the next morning by taking Runcible out of her cage and letting the parrot sit on her shoulder.

"Shut up!" said Runcible, sidling along Mattie's shoulder. She cocked her head and looked at the students. "Shut up please."

The noisy class quieted down.

"As you know," Matilda told them, "we have only two days until the Math Bee."

"I can't wait," said Julie.

Matilda ignored her. "We need to win the Math Bee, and to do that I've decided to bring in a math coach."

"You got a math genius to come coach us?" asked Ethan, incredulous. "How'd you do that?"

"What is he, a college professor or something?" asked Mollie.

Mattie smiled. "You remember I told you I had a secret weapon? I brought it with me today. Please meet my secret weapon."

She opened the door and gestured to someone in the

hall. A moment later, a lanky man with a silvery mustache and longish silvery hair stepped into the room.

"Wow. Albert Einstein," said one student.

"Looks just like him," said another.

Simon closed his eyes. It didn't look like Albert Einstein to him. It looked just like Uncle Philbert. Exactly like his great-uncle Philbert.

Maybe if he kept his eyes closed long enough, things would change. When he opened them again, Uncle Philbert would no longer be standing at the front of his class, reeking of barn, with little bits of hay sticking to his hair, his baggy farm overalls, his Bob's Feed Lot baseball hat. Sometimes wishes did come true, you know, if you closed your eyes and wished hard enough.

"Class, meet Mr. Philbert Maxwell," said Aunt Mattie to the students. And to Philbert she said, "Bertie, dear, we don't wear caps in the classroom."

"Are you a nuclear physicist?" asked Mario.

"No, sir," said Philbert pulling off his hat and picking some straw out of his mustache. "I'm a farmer."

There was an audible groan throughout the class. Students who had been sitting alertly in their seats slumped back in their chairs. Simon, who been slumping back in his chair to start with, slumped even lower. So much for wishing it all away. Never mind, he had a better plan: He could fake his own death. He would hold his breath for so long that he'd turn purple and they would call an ambulance and take him to a hospital. Preferably in Timbuktu.

"Excuse me," said Julie. "But why is a farmer coming

to coach us in arithmetic? Are you some sort of math brain?"

"Nope," said Philbert. "I hate math. Hated going to school. Hated all that stuff."

"Which is why he is the perfect person to *teach* you math," said Aunt Mattie. "I myself am quite good at math. Which means I'm no good at teaching it."

"Why?"

"Because, if you're very good at something, you can never understand people who have a hard time with it. Can't understand why they just don't get it."

"That's Mrs. Biggs," said Julie under her breath.

"No, what you need is not me but someone like Philbert."

"What you need," corrected Philbert, "is MultiQwik, Uncle Philbert's Patented Homework-Reducing Time-Saving Three-Step Multiple-Digit Multiplication Method.

"You see," he explained, "when I was your age, I hated wasting time on homework. Especially when there was really important stuff to be done, like collecting horse chestnuts or making turtle traps. So one day, kinda by accident, I discovered a much quicker way to do multiplication. It got me in a lot of trouble in school, because first they thought I was cheatin', then when they saw I wasn't cheatin' they got all upset. Decided my method was too different. They were scared of stuff that wasn't in their textbooks. So they didn't allow me to use it in school. But it sure made the homework go faster. And now I'm going to teach it to you."

"Do you need a computer?"

81

"How does it work?"

The class bombarded him with questions, but Philbert just shook his head.

"Hang on, young whiffets. Ask me a multiplication question. Two digits. Go ahead."

Mario pulled out a calculator. "Okay," he said. "What's 32 times 23?"

"Easy," said Philbert. "It's 736. Next question?"

"He's right," whispered Mario.

"What's 45 times 28?"

"Let's see." This time Philbert wrote the two numbers on the board, but instead of multiplying them out, he just looked at them. "I'm a little rusty," he explained. "That would be 1,260."

"Right again," said Mario. Simon let out his breath in a rush. The kids around him stopped fidgeting and sat up again in their seats. He decided to postpone dying for a little bit.

"Next question."

"What's up, doc?" (That was Runcible, and everyone ignored her, for once.)

"Can you do three digits?" asked Mario.

"Try me," said Philbert.

A half hour later, Uncle Philbert brushed the chalk dust off his hands, retrieved his cap, and faced Aunt Mattie.

"What do you think? Will they be able to do it?"

"I don't know," she said. "But at least now we've got a fighting chance. The proof, as they say, is in the pudding."

And the pudding, thought Simon, is the day after tomorrow. He looked around at the kids in his class. Not a lot of time to get ready. Not a lot of time at all.

To Bee or Not to Bee

$$165 \div 15 = ?$$
$$230 \div 12 = ?$$

The three fifth grades filed slowly into the auditorium ahead of the rest of the school and arranged themselves in the front rows. The teachers stood in groups at the rear of the room. As class monitor, Simon, too, stood at the rear of the room, for it was his job to do the overhead lights. Presently five students from each fifth-grade class climbed up onto the stage and took seats at one of three long tables. In the center of the stage was a blackboard, and Mr. Bickle, the principal, stood in front of it holding a sheaf of notes.

A few feet from Simon, Mr. Farley was whispering to Otis Lister. "Something's up," he said in a low voice.

"What do you mean?" asked the assistant principal.

"Look at that class, Mrs. Biggs's class. They're acting funny."

Simon looked. It was true. Instead of their habitual slouching, bored attitude, Mrs. Biggs's—Aunt Mattie's—students had exchanged high fives and were now making the thumbs-up sign to the five members of their class walking onto the stage.

"That's not possible. What is she thinking of?" Farley continued.

"What?"

"Look! Look at the kids she's picked for the Math Bee. I've got my best guys up there. But she's got—and where's Simon? He's the only smart kid in the class. He's not even up there. Sheesh. This is gonna be painful." He smirked.

Simon shrank back against the wall, hoping they wouldn't notice him. He thought back to the moment when Aunt Mattie had selected the math team. Simon had automatically stood up, pencil and paper in hand. He'd been on every Math Bee team this year.

"No, Simon, sit down," Aunt Mattie had said, looking around. "I think we'll have, let's see, Jimmy and Mindy and Raggie and Mollie, and . . . *Julie*." The looks on the faces of the five students had been almost comic: clearly they couldn't decide between shock, pride, and horror.

"Oh, goody," said Julie softly. "I just love public humiliation. It's so fun." For a long moment, Simon wondered if Julie would simply refuse to do it. He saw her look to Mollie and Mindy for support, but the two girls were bent over a sheet of paper. The other students were lining up to go.

"Come on," Simon had whispered to her. "You can do this." He grabbed a calculator. "I'll quiz you on the way." Julie had given him a look, half gratitude, half disbelief.

"This," she said as she snatched a pencil from her desk, "this is what you get when you have a fruitcake for a teacher."

Raggie, too, had looked terrified at being picked, and halfway to the auditorium he tried to bolt. But Jimmy collared him and dragged him back. "Cut it out, you little punk," he said fiercely. "If I can get up on that stage and make a fool out of myself, so can you. Besides," he added, "rocket scientists are supposed to be good at math."

Now here they all were, traipsing onto the stage, still looking slightly dazed, but definitely cheered by their classmates' show of confidence in them.

Mr. Bickle stood up to announce the rules of the Math Bee. Simon flicked the auditorium lights off and the stage lights on.

"As you know, the first person to . . . when you get the answer, as soon as you, you stand up and announce the answer. Five points for every correct answer, and two points off for every wrong, um, every one that's . . . Today we're doing division and multiplication. The winner is . . . the first team to get to one hundred is the, um . . . Are you ready?"

The students all nodded.

"Okay, here we . . . um . . . let's get . . . First question: 165 divided by 15 is . . . ?"

For the next fifteen minutes, as Mr. Bickle peppered them with long-division questions, Mr. Farley's and Miss Frescobaldi's teams battled it out.

"Look at that!" said Farley. "Mrs. Maxwell's class hasn't gotten a single answer—not a single point. This is embarrassing."

"You're wrong," hissed Mr. Lister. "They've gotten four points. *Minus* four points!" It was true. Mindy and Mollie had each tried to answer a question—with disastrous results. Still, the five of them sat up there looking remarkably calm. At the end of the first round of twenty questions, the score was Mr. Farley's class forty-eight points, Miss Frescobaldi's forty-two points, Matilda's minus six.

"Now we come to, it's time for the second half of, of . . ." announced Mr. Bickle. "Multiplication. Question number one: What is 43 times 12?"

Mindy stood up. At the other tables, students still busy scribbling on paper looked at her in surprise. Simon held his breath.

"Yes, Mindy?" said Mr. Bickle. "Are you, that is to say, do you have a question?"

"No," said Mindy. "I have an answer. Five hundred and sixteen." She sat down. Everyone stared, dumbfounded. Mr. Bickle consulted his notes. "Correct," he said slowly. "Very good, Mindy." He was too polite to say "Lucky guess," but Charley Farley wasn't.

"Dumb luck," said Mr. Farley with a laugh to Otis Lister. "Nearly lost the team another two points."

"Next question," continued Mr. Bickle: "What is 34 times 71?" This time there was a brief pause. Raggie jotted a few numbers on a sheet of paper and looked at Jimmy. "Go for it," muttered Jimmy. Raggie stood up. Once again, the other students stopped scribbling to stare.

"Can I help you, Raggie?" asked Mr. Bickle.

"No," said Raggie. "Two thousand four hundred and fourteen."

He sat down. Mr. Bickle consulted his notes.

"Correct," he said slowly, an astonished look on his face. "Raggie, that's, that's quite . . ."

"That's cheating, that's what it is," shouted Mr. Farley. "Nobody could get the right answer that fast." This time he said it so the whole auditorium could hear him.

"All right," said Mr. Bickle. "Quiet please"—for everyone was talking, including all the contestants. The only ones who were quiet were the five students from Matilda's class. They sat silently at their table, hands folded. Raggie and Mindy were even smiling and looking the tiniest bit smug.

"Next question: What is 84 times 79?"

This time it was Julie who stood up. Why'd she have to pick such a hard one? thought Simon. For the first time since he'd known her, she looked nervous in front of a crowd. Simon gave her a discreet thumbs-up and mouthed *Go on* at her. "Six thousand six hundred thirty-six," she said, and sat down. Simon checked his calculator: 6,636.

This time the auditorium erupted into cheers and shouts. Matilda's class was on its feet clapping. Mr. Farley ran down the aisle and bounded onto the stage.

"They're cheating," he announced. "Someone's got a calculator." To Mr. Bickle he said, "She told me she had a secret weapon."

But a quick search of the table revealed nothing but some paper and pencils—no secret weapon. Still Mr. Farley persisted. "Let me see your work," he said. "Look! There isn't any work. I told you they're cheating. They didn't even multiply the problem out. They just wrote down the answer." He held up a sheet. Indeed, he was right: Mindy's page contained nothing, not even the problem. Julie's and Raggie's contained only the problem written down, with the answer under it. "Someone must have copied your question sheet. They memorized the answers."

"Well, if you like I'll . . ." said Mr. Bickle, "I won't use my . . . I'll make up the next question on the, on the . . ."

"On the spot!" finished Mr. Lister for him. He, too, had climbed up on stage.

"And we'll have Mrs. Maxwell's class do the question

right here at the board," insisted Farley. "That way no one can possibly cheat."

Mr. Farley took a seat on the stage. Julie, Jimmy, Raggie, Mindy, and Mollie trooped obediently up to the blackboard.

"Okay, children," said Mr. Bickle, taking out a calculator, "the next problem is, um, let's see, 24 times 37." Simultaneously, Matilda's students wrote the problem on the board, while the others worked at their tables. More or less simultaneously, they all wrote the answer under the problem, without going through any of the usual steps for multiplying large numbers.

"I don't understand at all how you, what you . . ." said Mr. Bickle. "But you have all, you're all correct. You may sit down."

And so it went. Mr. Farley was, at last, speechless. Mr. Bickle rattled off the next questions, all made up on the spot. The students from Matilda's class were always first to answer, and were correct on all but two problems. Even when one of them got one wrong, someone else on the team jumped up with the right answer long before any other team was ready. Mr. Farley's class began making desperate attempts at wild guesses, only to lose points. When it was all over, Mattie's class had neatly beaten the others by more than fifty points. It was a rout.

And Mr. Farley's class had come in last.

Simon stood by the door waiting for the jubilant class to file out of the auditorium. Jimmy and Raggie walked by, both of them grinning. "Way to go," said

Simon. Raggie gave him a shy smile, and Jimmy turned and gave him a high five.

"Yeah," he said. "Way to go."

Simon was suddenly aware of Miss Frescobaldi, hovering by his side. She drew him away from the crowd of students.

"What's your secret weapon?" she asked Simon in a whisper. Even Miss Frescobaldi, it seemed, could not help feeling that some kind of, well, cheating must have gone on. So Simon explained to her, with the aid of a piece of paper and a pencil, Uncle Philbert's Patented Homework-Reducing Time-Saving Three-Step Multiple-Digit Multiplication Method.

"No secret weapon," he said. "Anyone can do it. Give me a problem."

"Um, 32 times 31," said Miss Frescobaldi. Simon nodded and wrote the following on the paper:

1. multiply	2. multiply and add results	3. multiply
3 2	3 2	3 2
$\updownarrow$	$\times$	$\updownarrow$
x3 1	x3 1	x3 1
2	9 2	992

"First you multiply the right-hand column of figures—that is the 2 and the 1. You get 2. Then you multiply each number diagonally and add them: so it's 1x3 plus 3x2, which equals 9. Then you multiply the left-hand column of figures: 3x3, which equals 9. There's your answer: 992. It gets a little harder if you have to carry a number, but you do that just like in adding. With a little practice you can do it all in your head, without any paper at all."

"How revolutionary," said Miss Frescobaldi. "I'm going to try it on my students right away. It's so easy!"

"Not to mention," said Simon, grinning, "extremely proficuous."

"So," he said to Julie when he finally caught up with the class. "You still think she's a fruitcake?"

"I'll give her this much," said Julie. "She's smart. A very smart fruitcake. But still a fruitcake. And Philbert's a nut." She looked around. "Get it? A *filbert* is a kind of nut. Hello? You're supposed to laugh, people."

But no one did. Julie's joke seemed forced, as if her heart wasn't really in it. And everyone else was busy talking about the Math Bee and making fun of the expressions on the faces of Mr. Farley and his class. Perhaps, thought Simon, laughing at subs had become old; but gloating about winning—now *that* was something new and different!

No Respect

PRINCIPAL
Otis T. Lister

Mr. Lister and Mr. Farley walked silently down the hall to Mr. Lister's office.

"Come into my office for a minute, Charley," said the assistant principal. He shut the door firmly behind them. "We've got to do something about that Maxwell woman," he said the moment the door clicked shut. "She has no respect for rules or authority. And she is making a mockery of school discipline, setting a terrible example for the children."

Mr. Farley nodded absently. "That Math Bee," he said. "She had to have cheated."

"I can't decide who is worse—that impossible woman, or our fearless leader Herbert J. Bickle, who refuses to sack her."

"I don't know," said Farley, smoothing back his dark hair. "You can't fire someone for winning a Math Bee." This was not the first time he had listened to Otis Lister complain about Mrs. Maxwell, or Mr. Bickle.

"They've got to go," sputtered Lister. "Both of them. And it's to your advantage, Charley, to see that they do go." This got Mr. Farley's attention.

"How so?" he asked, sitting up straight.

Mr. Lister swiveled his chair so that he was looking out the window.

"Imagine if you will—just hypothetically now—that Mr. Herbert J. Bickle was, unexpectedly, to lose his job. And imagine if you will that"—he cleared his throat a bit—"that Assistant Principal Otis T. Lister took his place. Well, that would leave open the job of assistant principal, wouldn't it? And *Principal* Otis T. Lister"— this had such a nice ring to it, he said it again— "Principal Otis T. Lister could think of someone who would make a very *good* assistant principal. Someone covered with the glory of winning yet another science fair, for example."

He spun his chair and looked straight at Mr. Farley, who jumped up and began to pace.

"Yes!" exclaimed Farley. "Someone who had brought honor—and prizes—showering down upon the school!"

"A proven winner," concluded Lister solemnly.

Mr. Farley stopped pacing. "But how?" he asked. "How do we get rid of Bickle?"

"Bickle is away next Wednesday," said Otis. "And while the cat's away . . ."

"What are you planning?"

"I happen to know that the superintendent of schools will be here that day. I've arranged for a special assembly, and I'm going to give a speech. I'm working on it right now." He patted a pile of papers on his desk. "It will display Herbert Bickle and Otis Lister in their true light." He straightened himself and gazed grandly out the window. Charley Farley could see that he was rehearsing some of the lines of that speech in his head. Otis Lister smiled and nodded to an imaginary audience. His lips moved silently. Suddenly the smile vanished and he returned to earth. "But that won't take care of the Maxwell woman. How are we to get rid of her?"

Mr. Farley had a quick inspiration. "Why are we worrying ourselves about her?" he asked. "The kids in her class will take care of her for us. They always do. I heard several of them placing bets on how many days she would last. No sub has ever lasted more than a week with that class."

"I hope you're right."

"I'm always right, Otis," he said with a laugh. "Trust me."

What the World Needs Now

"Well, we know we can win a Math Bee," said Aunt Mattie, regarding the class. "Now, on to the Science Fair. Let us find a project worthy of this class."

The students were still buzzing with pleasure and excitement at having won the Bee. But the mention of the Science Fair created complete silence.

"Julie, what do you like?"

"Huh?" said Julie. "What's that got to do with science? I'm no good at science. I hate it."

"Just like you're no good at math? Answer the question. Tell me what you *are* good at."

Julie made a face at Mindy. "Okay. Acting. Want to see my impersonation of Mr. Bickle?" She jumped up.

"I'd love to," said Matilda, making a note, "some other time, thank you. Now, Mindy. What do you like?"

"I like to write." Matilda noted this down.

"Mario? What are you good at?"

Mario raised his head from his desk and yawned. "Sleeping," he said. This got a laugh, but Matilda noted it down anyway.

"Moses?"

"Well," said Moses slowly, and a grin split his wide, round face. "Eating. Food. I like cooking and eating."

"Good. Sebastian?"

"I like to draw."

"Ethan?"

"I dunno. Building stuff, I guess. I like Legos."

"Raggie?"

"Rockets," said Raggie. "Real rockets."

And so it went around the room. Mandy liked her pet guinea pigs. Mollie liked rock music. Jimmy liked rocks. Bix liked basketball. At last she came to Simon.

"Simon, what do you like?"

"Math, I guess."

"Math. Anything else?"

"And my cat, Raspberry."

Aunt Mattie looked up.

"I see." There was a pause as she looked down at her notes. "Well, you all have a lot of things you're good at or you like. Which brings me to the last question: What do you hate?"

"That's easy," said Mario with another yawn. "Getting up in the morning."

"Yeah," chorused other students.

"And eating breakfast," added Mandy. "It's always the same thing—cold cereal."

"All right," said Matilda briskly. "This makes things easy. The world may not need another computer, but it clearly needs something to make it easier to get up in the morning and eat breakfast. Your assignment, then, for the weekend, is to design a machine, using the things you do like, to help with the things you don't like.

"Now let us turn to vocabulary. Who here knows what *pecksniffian* means? Nobody? What about *muculent*? Good. Write a definition for both of them."

The Mighty Muculent Egg Machine

Simon, his head bent over the desk, was grappling with the ignition problem, along with Raggie and Jimmy. Sebastian stood at the blackboard, drawing furiously as all around him students called out instructions. It was Monday morning, and Mrs. Maxwell was nowhere to be seen.

"It's going to be like *Scrambled Eggs Super*," said Mindy, waving the Dr. Seuss book in the air. "Only more super."

"It has to be taller, make it taller, Sebastian, so the eggs will break," said Ethan. "You need a ramp there, with a big drop."

"But what about the music?" asked Mollie. "How does that turn on?"

"Simple," said Jimmy. "Raggie's figured it out."

Raggie stood up bashfully. "With a rocket," he said.

"What?" shouted everyone, so Raggie ran to the board and demonstrated.

"Cool," said Ethan, and suddenly the whole class was talking at once. When at last Aunt Mattie walked in, a full forty-five minutes late, she was greeted with cries of

"We've got it!" and "We're ready," and "We're gonna blow them away!"

"Quiet, please," interrupted Matilda. "Everyone take your seats." Quiet—or something resembling quiet—fell, and the tangled mob of children gradually sorted itself into students who were more or less sitting at their desks.

"How does your corporosity seem to gashiate this morning?"

As usual there was no answer to this question, so she continued. "What have you been doing while I was late? Something interesting, I trust. Who would like to go first? Simon?"

"Go on, Simon," shouted Jimmy. "You explain it."

Simon stood up. "Well," he began, "we've thought up a project. For the Science Fair. Using the stuff we talked about on Friday—you know, using the stuff we like, to make something that solves a problem."

Aunt Mattie raised her eyebrows. "Indeed?"

"Yes," said Simon, and went to the front of the room. He picked up the pointer Mrs. Biggs had used for geography lessons. "It's called The Mighty Muculent Egg-Breaking and Breakfast-Making Morning-Waking Machine."

"I thought up the name," said Mindy.

"And the starring part will be played by *moi*," said Julie. She bowed to an imaginary audience. "Thank you, thank you very much."

"Please, Simon, go on."

"Here's how it works." Simon pointed to Sebastian's drawing on the blackboard and began to explain, using broad gestures and trying to ignore the students who interrupted him over and over, afraid he'd missed an important part.

"Well, I never," said Aunt Mattie when he was done. "Have you left anything out?"

"I don't think so," said Simon.

Matilda glanced at the notes she had taken on Friday. "Except possibly guinea pigs," she said. She smiled at the students. "And I'm sure you can find a way to fit them in."

Work began on the Mighty Muculent Egg Machine that very week—but not in the way Simon or anyone else had expected.

On Monday afternoon Mrs. Maxwell gave out warnings to everyone in the class who didn't already have them—for not being late enough that morning, she explained. A howl of protest erupted from everyone but Raggie.

"Two warnings!"

"Not fair!"

"We'll have to stay after school tomorrow."

"Yes, you will!" said Matilda happily. "I'm staying, too, of course: I've got three warnings, but I'm willing to share mine if somebody didn't get enough. Now, who will bring the popcorn?"

"Popcorn?"

"Yes. I myself will bring some of my famous raspberry-butterscotch cookies. And lemonade. I don't approve of soda. Now, then, volunteers for popcorn?"

As had happened so often in the last five days, the class regarded Mrs. Maxwell speechlessly.

"Why?" asked Jimmy at last.

"Why? For the party, of course," said Matilda. "You can't have a Detention Party without food. I would have thought that was obvious."

"Detention Party?"

"Yes, of course. Well, we can't let Raggie be the only one who gets to stay after school, can we? I'm sorry, Raggie, but you must share the fun with others."

A huge grin was spreading across Raggie's thin face.

"A party?" he said. "Cool. A party!"

"Yes," said Matilda. She glanced round the classroom. "And maybe—if you're good—maybe I'll let you all work on the Science Fair project. But only if you're good."

Mr. Farley shut the door to Otis Lister's office. "They've finally gotten to her," he said with a laugh. "Yes, she'll crack yet. Any day now."

"Why do you say that?" asked the assistant principal. "She looks quite cheerful every time I see her. Maddeningly cheerful. Horribly, infuriatingly cheerful."

Mr. Farley held up a fistful of pink slips. He flourished them in Mr. Lister's face. "Warnings. Detentions. She's been handing them out like confetti. Oh, yes. Any day now, she'll snap. I'm always right, Otis old boy. Did I mention to you that I'm always right? Why, the only time I've ever been known to be wrong was once in 1996 when I thought I had made a mistake—but I was mistaken." He laughed loudly. "Trust me on this, Otis. Just trust me."

Measure Twice, Cut Once

That Tuesday after school was to be the Detention Party.

Aunt Mattie brought the raspberry-butterscotch cookies that Simon remembered so well. And lemonade. Not regular yellow lemonade, or even pink lemonade, but blue lemonade because, as she explained, why not?

Bix and Julie brought trash bags filled with popcorn. Raggie brought rocket fuses and brownies he had convinced his older sisters to bake for him. Ethan brought a huge box of Legos. Moses brought eggs and a frying pan. Mandy brought her guinea pig. Jimmy brought his rock collection. Other children brought lumber scrounged from garages, hammers and tenpenny nails, pulleys, string, CD players, remote controls, eggbeaters, mixing bowls, batteries, wires, duct tape, and art supplies.

Outside, the sun was shining on a beautiful May day, but the children never once glanced out the window. They labored all afternoon on the Egg Machine. Matilda, who had a gift for machines (she had once,

Simon knew, rebuilt the engine of a 1946 New York taxicab all by herself) refused to participate. She claimed that this was the class's project and her role was to provide refreshments, encouragement, and first aid to children who insisted on hammering their fingernails instead of their tenpenny nails.

It was slow work, and frustrating. Simon, busy calculating the dimensions and angles of the machine, made a rare mathematical mistake and everyone had to redo a whole section.

"Measure twice, cut once," said Matilda from her desk, where she was peacefully knitting something that might have been a scarf for a smallish giraffe. "The motto of every good carpenter." And she said it more than once.

At another point, the structure, what little there was of it, collapsed under its own weight and needed to be completely rebuilt.

"Let us take a moment to consider how you calculate the weight-bearing capacity of the pulley," said Matilda. She went to the blackboard and drew some diagrams and formulas. The class watched silently while she explained. "Now have some lemonade, and start again."

By the end of the afternoon, two children had bandaged thumbs, three more had narrowly escaped stapling themselves to the floor, and almost all of them were covered in some combination of Elmer's glue, sawdust, and tempera paint. But a crude structure had taken shape on the floor of the classroom. It was far—very far—from being done. Nonetheless, it was an embryonic Egg Machine. Any fool could see that. Undeniably the beginning of the one and only Mighty Muculent Egg-Breaking and Breakfast-Making Morning-Waking Machine.

Weak Spot

Otis Lister grabbed Charley Farley as he walked past. He looked left and looked right, then opened the door to the staff bathroom and pulled Farley inside. He carefully locked the door behind him. "Charley," he hissed. "We need to talk."

"What's up?" asked Mr. Farley, looking around nervously.

"Did you realize that they were having a detention 'party' after school in Mrs. Maxwell's class?"

"A party?"

"Yes. I said something to Raggie this morning, something stern and fatherly, a shame he had to waste his time staying after school and so on. And he told me he had had *fun* in detention! They had a party—the whole class. *Awesome* was the word he used, I think. And they're doing it again tomorrow—all week in fact."

"But—" sputtered Mr. Farley.

"So much for your trust-me-I'm-never-wrong. Never ever wrong! 'Trust me on this, Otis old boy!' Huh! Well, we're in a fine mess. The kids won't drive Mrs. Maxwell away. And Mr. Bickle won't fire her. What do you suggest now, Mr. I'm Never Wrong?"

Farley had been looking crestfallen, but now he perked up.

"Wait a minute," he said. "We could make this work to our advantage. We'll go over Bickle's head—straight to his boss."

"The school board?"

"Somehow, somehow, we have to make the school board see that Mrs. Maxwell is a dangerous fool, a fruitcake—and that Bickle is an even worse fool for having hired her. Yes, that way we can kill two birds with one stone, get rid of her and Bickle at the same time. You could send the board a memo about Mrs. Maxwell, expressing some of your doubts about her—in the kindest, gentlest terms, of course."

Mr. Lister had recovered from his temper tantrum. He nodded.

"Yes, of course. But will that be enough? Don't they need evidence of what a bad teacher she is? Some proof?" He paced back and forth in the small room, trying to think, the speech he was about to deliver momentarily forgotten. Suddenly Charley smiled.

"I've got it," he said. "The Science Fair."

Mr. Lister looked at him quizzically.

"The Science Fair?"

"Yes," said Farley, and he was laughing now. "Don't you see? Her class is bound to turn in something laughable, embarrassingly awful—they've scrapped Mrs. Biggs's project, with only a few weeks to go until the fair. And anything that class produces is bound to be rotten. By contrast," he added, "my project, I mean my *class*'s project, is brilliant—so brilliant that hers will look even more pathetic by comparison. Trust me on this, Otis. Haven't I told you, I'm always right!" He peered at himself in the mirror, straightened his tie, and smoothed back his hair.

"But how does that help us?"

"Don't you see? All the fifth-grade parents will be at the Science Fair, and it just so happens—"

"—that two of those parents are on the school board!" finished Lister for him, with a laugh. "Brilliant, Charley. And I'll see to it that the superintendent comes, too. All you have to do is win. All right, I like this plan." A small frown furrowed his brow. "Though I'd be a lot happier if I knew for sure what her science project was."

"Yes," said Farley. "You're right." Suddenly he smiled. "Don't worry, Otis. I've got it. They have a weak spot. And I think I know how to make the most of it."

"Do what you need to do, Charley. We can't let anything stand in our way," said Otis. "Not anything. Now I have a speech to give."

A minute after Mr. Farley and Mr. Lister left the bathroom, the door to the second stall opened slowly. A tousled head peered out. Then a slim form opened the bathroom door, looked both ways, and bolted.

Who You Callin' a Fruitcake?

"Listen up," said Jimmy. "Raggie has something important to say."

The whole class was gathered on the playground behind the swings. Jimmy gave Raggie a shove. "Go on. Tell them what you heard."

"They're going to get Mrs. Maxwell fired," said Raggie. "Mr. Lister and Mr. Farley. They say she's a fruitcake."

Well, thought Simon, they got what they wanted. Why aren't they cheering? For that matter, why wasn't *he* cheering? With Aunt Mattie gone, his life would be simple again.

But instead of cheers, a silence settled on the group. Then Ethan pulled his yo-yo out of his pocket. He handed it to Julie.

"Looks like you win," he said. Julie didn't move.

"Sink the Sub," explained Mindy. "Remember? It's been only a week, and she's out of here." She pulled her eraser from her pocket and held it out. Julie stared at the yo-yo and the eraser. Then Jimmy pushed through the kids to stand beside her.

"They can't fire Mrs. Maxwell," he said fiercely. "She's *our* sub. Right?"

Julie looked around at the other kids. "Right," she said slowly. She pushed the yo-yo and the eraser away. "And *no one* calls our sub a fruitcake. No one." She smiled at Jimmy. And then everyone else, Simon included, took up the cry: "Yeah," they shouted. "No one fires our sub but *us*."

Julie turned to Raggie. "Okay, Raggie," she said. "Tell us everything you know."

Permission to Breathe

"It has come to my attention," said Mr. Lister, "that you have been conducting science experiments in your classroom."

"Yes," said Matilda, hurriedly putting Runcible back in her cage and locking her door. Ever since their first encounter, Runcible had taken a strong dislike to Mr. Lister. Parrots can do that. Some people they love at first sight, others they hate. And like elephants, they live a long time and have very long memories. Once a parrot has decided that you are dog meat, it's all over for you. "Behave yourself, you reprobate," Matilda warned.

"I beg your pardon?" asked Mr. Lister, with a deeply offended expression on his face.

"I was addressing the parrot, dear boy."

"Oh. Well, as I said, you are doing science experiments in the classroom." He surveyed the empty room—it was recess time, the children were outside. At the back of the room, the embryonic Egg Machine was covered with a blue plastic tarp, to protect it from prying eyes. "By the way, what exactly is it that you are doing for the Fair?"

"I'm afraid that's classified as Top Secret," said Matilda. "The children have the strange notion that if word gets out, it may be sabotaged."

"Sabotaged? How absurd! How ridiculous! I merely asked from curiosity. I am sure it is a very fine and laudable—"

"Yes," said Matilda proudly. "It's a humdinger. A lollapaloosa. They've a good chance for a prize."

Mr. Lister produced a huge sheaf of papers. "Yes, I'm sure," he said with another curious glance in the direction of the tarp. "However, I must ask, have you had the children and their parents sign a consent form?"

"We need their consent to do science experiments?" asked Matilda, incredulous.

"Of course you do. School policy. We could be sued. Here are the papers. No more experiments until every student and every parent has signed one of these and brought it back to the office."

Matilda looked at the paper. "Permission to Conduct Science Experiments. I find this hard to believe."

"Times have changed since you were in school," said Lister flatly. He produced a second batch of papers. "And if you are conducting class after school hours, you will need to have students and their parents—both parents—read and sign these papers as well."

He handed Matilda a batch of three-page sheets entitled Extracurricular Policy and Procedures for Alcohol and Drugs.

"But we are not using alcohol or drugs in our experiment."

"I should hope *not*! But the students need to sign a form saying they will refrain from alcohol or drugs while participating in extracurricular activities."

"I see. Are popcorn and lemonade okay?"

Lister ignored her.

"And these." Another three-page sheet labeled Standards of Behavior for Participating in Extracurricular Activities. "This explains what is and isn't acceptable behavior on school grounds."

"My dear Mr. Lister, I think I can explain that to the students perfectly well."

"We need a signed form. School policy. And these, too." A two-page sheet: Contract for Science Fair Behavior. "That explains that if you cheat on the project you automatically get a zero."

"I should have thought that was obvious. Anything else?"

"Well, that pretty much covers science and extracurricular activities."

"Don't they need to sign a form saying they will not manufacture bombs during science lab?"

"This is not a joking matter," said Lister sternly. "But, now that you mention dangerous experiments, it has come to my attention, via the school nurse, that two children required medical attention as a result of your science experiment."

"Yes, if you consider an ice cube medical attention. Poor things. Two of them seemed to think that the point of our experiment was to prove that if you hit your thumb with a hammer, it would hurt like the dickens. I applied some ice."

"Again, no joking matter." He produced another sheaf of papers. "You will need to fill out these forms in triplicate for each child who was injured and have them signed by the school nurse and all the parents involved."

Matilda looked at them. School Accident Report Form. "But I sent a note home to their parents explaining what happened."

"Not good enough. Lawsuits, don't you know. Lawsuits. And all the children's parents will have to sign these forms as well. I understand you applied Band-Aids to the two fingers in question?"

"Yes. They didn't really need them, but have you ever

noticed how children seem to find it comforting to have a Band-Aid applied?"

"No, I haven't. And you—"

"Especially if it has dinosaurs or rocket ships on it. These had dinosaurs. Oh, and I gave one child an aspirin."

"Very bad!" said Lister. "Very wrong. Illegal, in fact."

"He had a headache. Oh dear. Must I file a copy of the School Headache Report Form?"

"The problem is, we did not have on file a copy of this"—he produced another piece of paper—"signed by the parent: Permission to Administer Medications."

Matilda smiled at the papers. "Do I need to have them all notarized? Witnessed? Approved by the President?"

"No," said Lister, who did not appear to notice her attempt at humor. "Just the parents. But this separate page, Physician Consent Form, must also be signed by each child's personal doctor. In the future, you may not administer any medications, even aspirin or aspirin substitutes, without a signed copy of both these forms. Is that quite clear?"

Matilda looked at the huge stack of papers he had placed on her desk.

"Whatta loada baloney."

As usual, it was Runcible. Having the last word. Matilda glared at her.

"Runcible, say you're sorry," she said sternly.

Runcible cocked her head and looked straight at Mr. Lister.

"You're sorry," Runcible said. "You're very sorry."

117

Pecksniffian

"Rodomontade, rodomontade," said Otis Lister, thumbing through the dictionary. He looked up as Charley Farley entered his office.

"Charley. Do you have any idea what *rodomontade* means?"

"No," said Farley. "Funny—I was just going to ask you what *pecksniffian* means. Do you know?"

"No," said Lister. "Why?"

"Well, I caught that pest Raggie in the library without a hall pass, trying to cut *your* assembly—"

"As per usual. Did you give him a warning?"

"You remember what I told you about that class having a weak spot? Well, Raggie's it. I happen to know that Raggie can't afford to get any more detentions. I realized this was my perfect opportunity to pump him about the Science Fair project."

"Good thinking!"

"So I asked him how it was going. 'Just fine,' he says. 'If you tell me about it,' says I, 'perhaps I can give you a little guidance. See if you're headed down a blind alley, that sort of thing. Save you making mistakes, wasting your time.' "

"Very generous of you, Charley. Very selfless."

"Exactly. Well, that's the sort of person I am. Selfless. Not asking for thanks. But what do you think this wretched boy says to that offer? 'No, thanks,' says he. 'I'm not supposed to discuss the project.' Can you imagine that? And so I decide to give him that warning for not having a hall pass after all, when suddenly Jimmy pops up—I don't know where *he* came from—and says, 'But it was very pecksniffian of you to offer, sir.' 'Yes,' says Raggie. 'Very pecksniffian.' Well, what could I do? I patted him on the head and tore up the warning, then and there."

"Of course. Anyone would have done the same."

"But now I have to look up that word." He reached for the dictionary. "Let me have a quick look. I'm late for lunch duty."

"Sure, here. Funny, it was another one of Mrs. Maxwell's kids who used the word *rodomontade*. I was just going to look it up now. She used it after this morning's assembly. All modesty aside, I thought that was a pretty rousing speech I gave, eh, Charley? About everything I've done for this school. Perhaps I blew my own horn a bit too much. . . ." Here he paused to give Mr. Farley the opportunity to disagree, which Mr. Farley obligingly did.

"Not at all, not at all. We mustn't hide our light under a bushel, my mother always used to say. If we don't sing our own praises, who will?"

"Exactly my line of thought. Bickle would never go

out of his way to sing *my* praises. I doubt he even knows I really exist. The students need to realize how lucky they are to be in a school with an assistant principal who cares about standards and policies and discipline . . ."

"Absolutely. Especially discipline."

"And if there happened to be a few parents and the superintendent of schools in the audience that morning, as luck would have it, well, what harm could it do for them to know the truth about who is the real strength behind this school administration?"

Farley looked up from the dictionary. "Harm? Well, I should think quite the opposite. It's high time they knew what a broken reed Herbert J. Bickle is."

"Yes. A broken reed. Really, completely hopeless, that man. Anyway, afterward that girl, what's her name, Julie. The wise-mouth."

"The one who calls you 'Mr. Listerine' behind your back?"

Otis Lister made a sour face. "The same. Well, she came up to me just now with a big smile and said she thought my speech had been quite a rodomontade. I thanked her."

"Quite right," said Farley.

"I must admit"—here he smiled modestly—"I felt it was quite an accomplishment that a humble little speech of mine could make such a deep impression on a hopeless child like that. It was a good speech, though, wasn't it? You don't think I was overreaching just a little when I said that bit about how the 'flower of our youth must be planted with a firm hand in the garden of—'"

120

"The devil!" said Farley.

"No, it wasn't the garden of the devil. It was—"

"I mean Raggie. And Jimmy. Those devils. Why, that little wretch!"

"What is it? What's wrong?"

Farley handed the dictionary back to Lister. He pointed to the definition of *pecksniffian*.

" 'Selfish and corrupt, behind a false display of good-will,' " read Mr. Lister. "Good lord. What cheek. What nerve. You must send him to the principal's office at once."

"How can I?" sputtered Farley. "I already thanked him for the compliment." He paced angrily back and forth in the cramped office. A sudden thought occurred to him. "You'd better look up rodo-whatever-it-is."

"Rodomontade," said Mr. Lister slowly. A deep red flush was creeping into his cheeks. "I've just found it." Mr. Farley looked over his shoulder, and read aloud:

" 'Rodomontade. Vain boasting or bluster. A bragging speech.' "

A silence fell. The two men looked at each other. Finally Mr. Lister slammed the dictionary shut.

"That tears it," he said. "Someone has to teach that class a lesson. They are out of control."

"No one can get away with rudeness like that."

"Somehow, I don't know why, but I suspect Mrs. Maxwell is behind all this. She has no sense of respect for authority. None. Not like Mrs. Biggs did. Now *there* was a woman who knew how to keep kids in line. Did I tell you that Mrs. Maxwell once tried to send *me* to the principal's office?"

"Yes," said Mr. Farley. "Many times."

"We must show her up before she makes a laughing-stock of us."

"The Science Fair," said Farley.

"Yes," said Mr. Lister slowly. "The Science Fair."

The Funny Farm

The Field Trip Permission slips were all in order. The yellow school bus was waiting. The Mighty Muculent Egg Machine was packed up and ready to travel. And Simon's stomach was in a knot.

Miss Frescobaldi saw him in the office, delivering the attendance sheet. "Off on a field trip?" she inquired. "I suppose this is your prize for winning the Math Bee? The day off from school."

"Yes," said Simon. "We're going to visit a working farm."

"Anything to get them out of the classroom," said Miss Frescobaldi to the school secretary, with a knowing look. "The students are so hard to control at this time of year. Summer beckons."

"No," Simon said. "We're field-testing our Science Fair project." I just wish we didn't have to test it at this particular farm, he added to himself. At that moment his class filed by on their way to the bus.

"You're testing the egg machine?" Miss Frescobaldi asked Matilda.

"It's supposed to be a secret," Matilda said to her.

"The children are convinced that someone will try to sabotage it if word gets out what we are making."

Miss Frescobaldi made the gesture of zipping her lips, locking them, and throwing away the key. "Not another word about it," she said. "I wish you the best of luck. Bring me back some farm-fresh eggs."

"Duck or peacock?" asked Matilda.

Miss Frescobaldi laughed. "Peacock, of course."

But Simon knew that Aunt Matilda had been quite serious.

Not long afterward the bus pulled into the dusty driveway of Matilda's farm and came to a stop at the rambling red farmhouse that Simon knew and loved so well. But on this day the sight of the farm filled him with anxiety.

Little had changed since his last visit. There were the peacocks on the roof, still; the motorcycle and bed frame in the yard, still; the dozens of cats lounging in the shade of the front veranda, as always. The daffodils in the flower boxes had been replaced with red geraniums, but they were being eaten, as usual, by Sugar, the sway-backed white horse. In the paddock behind the barn Simon could see Uncle Philbert performing some chore. He, along with the three llamas roaming the paddock, came and leaned against the fence for a closer look at the schoolchildren piling out of the bus.

Scuffing around the dirt in front of the barn was a funny-looking black-and-white-flecked hen that Simon had never seen before. It made an extraordinary noise—something like a turkey with a bad case of the hiccups.

"I didn't think you had chickens," said Simon to Aunt Mattie.

Julie looked at him with her funny, half-closed-eyes look. "How would you know?" she asked.

"Well," said Simon, flustered, "I mean, they don't seem like the kind of animal Aun—Mrs. Maxwell would have. They're too . . . too useful. None of the other animals are very useful." Julie gave him another Look.

"Simon's right," said Aunt Mattie quickly. "I generally only like animals other people don't want because they aren't useful, or because they've outlived their usefulness. Peacocks, for instance, don't do anything useful, but they are so lovely to look at. Kind of like beautiful flowers that come to life and make ugly noises.

"No, I acquired Henrietta here—and she's actually a guinea hen—because when chickens get to a certain age, they stop laying eggs regularly. Then they get made into chicken stroganoff or something, and that never seemed to me to be a good reward for having spent your life providing breakfast for people.

"Now the funny thing is that, much as I love animals, I can't get them to behave at all. Even Runcible, isn't that right, Runcible?" She addressed the parrot in her cage.

"Get over it," said Runcible with a flap of her wings.

"You see what I mean? I can make any kind of machine work—cars, motorcycles, lawnmowers—but animals, well, I leave that to Uncle Philbert. The animals love him. Even Henrietta started laying again when he got his hands on her."

It was true. Though Aunt Mattie loved all kinds of animals, and collected and rescued huge numbers of them, on the whole they declined to treat her with the respect she deserved. The stray cats she took in from the cold howled in protest if she should go so far as to tread or sit upon them, as she frequently did. The llamas, far from being grateful to her when she fed them, often rewarded her for her troubles with a nip. The horses, saved from the glue factory, refused, simply refused, to do a single thing she asked of them, planting their feet like mules when she tried to push or pull them in a given direction. Even ducks and chickens scattered at her approach.

But Uncle Philbert—that was another story entirely. The horses gentled under his touch, the llamas became absolutely bashful, the ducks practically ran up to sit in his lap, and the cats purred with contentment whenever he was near.

"Tosh," said Philbert, coming around the corner with a bucket of hen food. "All I did to Henrietta was give her some vitamins and calcium. That's all she needed." He scooped her up and stared her in the face. "And a little encouragement. A pep talk. Right, Henny Penny?"

Aunt Mattie left the class in Uncle Philbert's care while she went indoors. He showed the children around the farmyard. Simon hung back to the rear of the group, and when they approached the llamas he took special care to stay out of sight. The last time he'd been here, during spring vacation, the biggest one, Mr. Ugly, had taken a strong dislike to him (having something to do with a spitting contest, about which the less said the better). Llamas, like parrots, had long memories and Simon was not anxious for Mr. Ugly to demonstrate that they were old friends—or rather old enemies.

But the llamas—perhaps because of Uncle Philbert's influence—were on their best behavior today. They allowed Mindy and Mandy and Mollie to stroke them, and they didn't seem to mind being told they had beautiful big eyes or lovely eyelashes. Then Philbert introduced the children to a few of the cats. "This one here," he said, undraping a limp white cat from its warm perch on a bale of hay and passing it around, "is Priscilla Goodcat. Most useless varmint ever invented, a complete waste of oxygen. Why, she couldn't catch a mouse if it walked into her mouth and down her throat. And this one"—he picked up a striped tomcat—"is B. Bobbin Badcat. Another waste of cat food. Thinks his job is to be on the wrong side of a door. Yup, never met a door he didn't want to be on the other side of . . ."

Fortunately, Mr. Ugly never caught wind of Simon, and Simon was beginning to relax when somebody said, "Hey, look, there's another horse, out in the pasture. Can we go see him, Mr. Maxwell?"

Uncle Philbert surveyed the group of children. "Even better," he said, "let's call him in. Is there anyone here who can whistle with their fingers?" Silence. Everyone looked at everyone else.

"Tarnation, what's the world comin' to?" asked Uncle Philbert crossly. "What do they teach you in school these days?"

127

Jimmy turned to Simon. "What about you?" he said. "I thought you said you had just learned to whistle. Your uncle taught you or something."

"Yuh, okay," muttered Simon. "It's just I'm not very good." But he placed his fingers to his mouth and gave a short, extremely good, whistle. As Simon had known he would, the chestnut horse at the far end of the pasture jerked his head up, listened a second, and cantered over to them. The moment Hero—for that was his name—saw Simon, he whinnied, stuck his head over the fence, nuzzled Simon's chest with his head, and began nibbling at his shirt pockets.

"Hey, stop that," said Simon, blushing.

"Wow," said Julie. "You'd think he knew you or something. What's he doing?"

"I believe," said Uncle Philbert, pulling some carrots out of his pocket, "he's looking for these." He passed the carrots out among the students, being sure to press several extra ones into Simon's hand.

Julie looked right at Simon. "You *sure* he doesn't know you?" she asked.

At that moment Aunt Mattie returned, puffing and extremely red-faced. "I can't catch that blasted hen for the life of me," she said. "She won't hold still for one second."

"Now why do you want to do that?" asked Philbert.

"We have to try out our Egg Machine," said Mattie. "It's time to stop playing and get down to work."

"You're right. It's time for some lessons," said Philbert. "This is supposed to be an educational field trip, ain't it? All play and no work makes Jack a dull boy and Jill a dull girl. For starters it is impossible to chase animals without first learning to whistle." So he administered lessons in whistling with your fingers. After twenty minutes, there were a large number of very dizzy children, and a small number who could make some faint, watery whistling noises through their fingers. After that he taught the children how to make owl and whippoorwill calls by blowing into their cupped hands. And having done that, he said it was only natural that they brush up on their ability to make duck calls using a blade of grass between their thumbs.

Once they were done with these lessons he announced that it was time to scientifically test the principles of skipping stones on the duck pond. To his horror, there were children who did not know how to skip stones.

"What's the world comin' to?" he asked again peevishly. "Now look here, you young whiffet. What's your name?"

"Julie."

"You throw a stone like that, it's not gonna skip. It's gonna sink like a, like a—"

"Like a stone?" offered Julie.

"Yep, like a stone. Now, you gotta cock your arm like this."

Julie gave it another try. Uncle Philbert looked disgusted.

"Did anyone ever tell you you throw like a girl?"

Julie looked at him coolly. "I am a girl," she said. Simon grinned. Uncle Philbert, well known to be one of the rudest men on earth, might have met his match.

"Nothin' we can do about that unfortunate fact," said Philbert calmly. "But just mebbe we can teach you to skip stones."

Within fifteen minutes, all the children in the class had mastered the scientific principles of skipping stones. Even Julie got one to skip a half-dozen times. Then Uncle Philbert called a halt and announced that it was time to scientifically test the temperature of the water in the pond.

And so the Egg Machine was forgotten while the children changed into bathing suits and spent the rest of the morning chasing ducks, getting muddy, swimming, getting muddy, and swimming. Afterward they ate lunch on the veranda.

When the last lunch box had been put away, Aunt Mattie said, "Now, can we catch that miserable hen?"

"You leave that to me, Mattie," said Philbert. And he hitched up his pants, strode off to the barnyard, and returned in five minutes with the guinea hen tucked under his arm, gurgling contentedly. (The hen, that is, not Philbert.)

"I declare, you are a magician with animals, Bertie. I must have chased that foolish fowl for fifteen minutes."

"You stick to machines," said Philbert, "and leave the animals to me." He patted the hen on the head. "Ain't that right, Henny Penny? Now where's this infernal contraption?"

The infernal contraption, as Philbert was to refer to it henceforward, had been set up on the back porch. With the guinea hen still tucked under his arm, Philbert walked all around it, peering suspiciously.

"I don't trust it," he said. "Doesn't look safe."

He reached out his free hand to touch it.

"No!" shouted Simon, and immediately got flustered. Everyone turned to look at him. "I mean, I mean—"

"The boy's quite right," said Aunt Mattie, jumping to his aid. "Keep your cotton-pickin' hands off it." She turned to the startled class to explain what Simon already knew. "Mr. Maxwell may be good with animals, but he is death to machines. Death. One touch and it's all over. *Finito*. Kaput. Sayonara."

Simon knew from personal experience that she was not exaggerating. He had seen Uncle Philbert destroy machines ranging from toasters to one-ton farm tractors. Sometimes, it seemed, he just had to look at them sideways for them to fall apart. Why, the dishwasher in Mattie's kitchen had been put permanently out of order by a single well-meaning attempt on Philbert's part to clean out the filter. (The next time they had run it, the plates and cups had emerged as thousands of small fragments of glass and china. It was now used as Mattie's desk and bookshelf.) On another occasion Simon had personally witnessed Philbert disable a sports car by simply laying his hands on the hood of the car. Fried the solenoid, just like that.

"Well," said Philbert, with a hurt look, "no need to be rude, you know. I was only tryin' to help."

"Well, dear, why don't you limit yourself to convincing Henrietta to lay an egg so we can try out our contraption here? It's all plugged in and ready to go."

"I don't know," said Philbert, stroking Henrietta's head. "She's quite unpredictable."

But he put her in the nest box at the top of the Egg Machine, bent over, and murmured a few words in her ear. Henrietta responded by ruffling up her feathers, making a few happy hiccuping sounds, and settling herself down into the straw.

"Cluck," she said, quite clearly, and then cocked her head to one side, looking at Philbert with her beady bright eyes.

"Go ahead," said Philbert. "Turn it on. She's ready. Or as ready as she'll ever be."

So they turned it on. There were, of course, a few bugs that needed working out. Once, when it seemed they were finally about to get it running, Uncle Philbert insisted on helping out by tightening a small screw. The "infernal contraption" instantly stopped and had to be completely recalibrated. After a few of these trial runs—or, rather, trial-and-error runs—everything and everyone got thoroughly covered in egg yolk, egg white, and scrambled egg. But they got back on the bus two hours later, tired and happy, if a bit, well, muculent.

Just Too Weird?

CLUCK

The Science Fair was held in the giant gymnasium of a local high school. Twenty fifth grades from seven schools around the county were there. The place was crammed with people looking frightfully busy and frightfully scientific. There were students and teachers, parents and principals, judges and onlookers.

They had been there bright and early setting up displays explaining the principles of composting and computing, photosynthesis and photography, geography and geology, the life cycle of plants, the social system of ants, fossils and missiles, water pollution, the moon's revolutions around the earth, the earth's revolutions around the sun, meal worm digestion and traffic congestion, and much much more. All of which Simon had seen in one form or another at every science fair he had ever been to.

The only thing that wasn't there was the Mighty Muculent Egg Machine. Simon was not worried about that—Aunt Mattie was always late. What did worry him, though, more and more as he wandered up and down the aisles looking at the other exhibits, was that none of the displays remotely resembled his class's project. Trust his class and Aunt Mattie to come up with something that no one had ever done before. Would everyone make fun of the Egg Machine? Would they be a laughingstock? Why had nobody stood up and said, "Hey, this is just too weird"? Because no one had ever stopped to think about it, that's why. Because everyone—even diehards like Julie and Jimmy—had been having too much fun doing it. But now it was Truth Time. And Truth Time looked like it might be painful.

Suddenly Simon stopped. He had come to the exhibit of Mr. Farley's class. At least fifty students were clustered around a big, professional-looking three-sided display. The printing on the board had been done in large, sophisticated type with computer-generated color graphics. It read:

Working Home Computer
It adds! It subtracts! It divides! It multiplies!
Constructed by
Mr. Charles Farley's Fifth Grade
(Defending State Champions)
Check it out!!!

Simon pushed through the kids waiting to try the computer. On the table was a plain, crude computer with a keyboard (very like one Simon had seen at Pflummerfield Electronics the other day) and a single logic board open for viewing. It was hooked up to a television screen, instead of a monitor—to make it look more homemade, Simon guessed. But surely the judges wouldn't be fooled. Would they?

Simon stood around for a while, watching the other kids use the computer, listening to their comments. "Awesome" was the one he heard most often, followed by "You guys really made this yourselves?" and "You're gonna win first prize for sure."

Suddenly he heard a commotion by the entry to the gym. It was Aunt Mattie and Uncle Philbert, making their way through the crowd, followed by a number of students lugging heavy cardboard boxes containing the disassembled Egg Machine. Much of the commotion was caused by Runcible, who was sidestepping up and down Mattie's shoulder, squawking, whistling, flapping her wings, and calling out loudly, "Heave-ho, mateys! Heave-ho! Wrawk. Outta my way, dog breath. Make a lane there. Make a lane."

"Oh, you jackanape!" cried Mattie, as Runcible's

claws dug into her neck. "Hold still. That hurts, you miserable miscreant."

"Thank you," said Runcible. "Please. Say thank you. Say please."

"Come to Papa," said Uncle Philbert, taking the parrot, who immediately calmed down and began nibbling his ear. "Mebbe you should've left her at home."

"The children wouldn't let me. They say she's their mascot."

"Do you hear that, Runcible?" said Philbert. "You're the class mascot. Now, you gotta make us proud of you."

Runcible, who was clearly feeling very nautical—not to mention naughty—stood at attention on Philbert's shoulder and suddenly began singing snatches of a sea chantey that was so rude it would have made even a sailor blush.

"Heave-ho, haul away for Rosie-o," she began in a surprisingly good voice. "Behind the pub with her—"

But evidently even Philbert had had enough. He plucked the parrot from his shoulder, and as soon as they got to their booth he deposited her in the cage. This he put under the table, next to the cardboard cat-carrying box that held Henrietta the guinea hen. "Perhaps you can teach Runcible some manners, Henny," he said.

The crowd around Simon had gradually become aware of the commotion surrounding the new arrivals, and they turned from the computer display to watch. "What a circus," said one parent. "Whose class is that?"

"It's Mrs. Maxwell and her Mighty Muculent Men," said Wilton Pflummerfield, and the kids around him snickered. Simon was reminded of Julie's Parallel Universe theory. Here it was all over again. Somehow Aunt Mattie had worked her magic on them, made them all think her brand of lunacy, their science project, their Egg Machine, was fine and possible, a winner even. But now, exposed to the harsh light of the every-day world—the Real Universe—it appeared ridiculous, absurd, embarrassing. How could this be?

"Why are you looking so gloomy?" said a voice beside him. It was Julie. Simon didn't answer right away.

"I was thinking about the Egg Machine," he said at last. "We're going to get laughed right out of the Science Fair, aren't we?"

"Hey," said Julie, "have you forgotten that it stars the great Julie Biedermeyer?" She made a grandiose gesture, and Simon managed a grin.

138

"Maybe that's exactly what I meant," he said. Julie laughed, and then turned serious.

"So maybe we will get laughed at," she said. "So who cares?" She gave him a funny look. "Maybe sometimes you just have to believe in something, no matter how weird it looks to other people, you know?"

Simon stared at her. "What do you mean?"

But before she could answer, Mindy showed up, saying they had to get the display set up. They hurried over to their table. Instantly, Mr. Lister appeared, with a clipboard in his hand.

"You're late," he said. "You were supposed to have been all set up by now. The judging starts soon."

"That's good," said Matilda. "Being late adds to the suspense, don't you think? Everyone must be asking themselves, Where oh where is the Mighty Egg Machine?"

"This is not a drama contest, Mrs. Maxwell. It is a Science Fair." Mr. Lister pressed his lips together and glanced down at his clipboard. "You are scheduled to give your presentation in fifty-five minutes. If you are late for *that*, you are disqualified. Dis-qual-i-fied," he repeated.

Each class had just ten minutes to explain their project to the judges and demonstrate how it worked. All morning the judges and other students had had a chance to cruise around looking at all the displays. But the actual demonstration was crucial—especially for the Mighty Muculent Egg-Breaking and Breakfast-Making Morning-Waking Machine, since it could actually function only once, using an egg from Henrietta. The rest of the time, it had to just sit there. For this reason, the class had decided to keep the machine hidden behind a curtain until the moment of the demonstration. To add to the suspense. All there was to see at this point was a large poster, hand drawn by Sebastian, with text by Mindy. Yesterday Simon had thought it was brilliant. Today, compared to Mr. Farley's display, it looked baby-ish and crude.

While Matilda's class was setting up, Mr. Farley and several of his students came by to watch.

"May I help in any little way?" offered Mr. Farley, gaz-ing curiously at the poster. Simon noticed Wilton Pflummerfield trying to see behind the curtain. "I real-ize you are a little behind schedule, and we have some time to spare."

"The children feel particularly strongly that they must do every aspect of the project without grown-up help. Even I am not allowed to assist," said Matilda. "That way they can really say it is their own work, how-ever flawed. I'm sure you understand."

Mr. Farley flushed but kept his smile in place. "Sure," he said. "Very honorable. My students have the same policy. The same. Don't we, kids?" The students, who'd been busily examining the booth area, looked up.

"Hunh?" said Wilton. "Oh, um, yeah. Yeah. We worked real hard on our project, and we're going to kick butt."

"Yes?" said Mrs. Maxwell kindly. "Go on. You're going to kick, but what?"

"No, I meant, kick, you know, kick . . ." Suddenly he got flustered and couldn't finish his sentence.

"So," said Mr. Farley, looking at the poster. "It's a Mighty Muculent Egg-Breaking and Breakfast-Making Morning-Waking Machine, eh, 'featuring Henrietta the Heroic Hen'? Sounds more like a science-fiction movie than a science project."

"It's a little of everything, actually," said Mattie.

"What on earth *is* it? And more to the point, what scientific principles does it demonstrate?"

"Goodness, I suppose it shows that when children put their minds to something, they can—"

"Cluck!"

"Cluck?" Mr. Farley bent over and looked under the table. Henrietta poked her head through a hole in the cat box. "Cluck!" she repeated. From her cage next door, Runcible gave the hen a dirty look and said, "Shut up. Say thank you. Get a life."

Mr. Farley straightened up, a condescending smile on his lips. The other students were clearly trying to keep themselves from laughing.

"This I've got to see," said Mr. Farley.

"Come back at 1:15 and you will," said Matilda tartly.

"I wouldn't miss it for the world," he said, and laughed.

"I agree," said a man who had been listening to the conversation. "I wouldn't miss it for the world, either."

The strange man stepped forward toward the booth, and Simon saw for the first time that he wore a blue ribbon on his lapel, labeled JUDGE.

The smile faded from Mr. Farley's face. He quickly arranged his features into an expression of sincere respect and held out his hand.

"Very pleased to meet you," he said quickly, pumping

the man's hand. "Charles Farley. I do so hope you'll have a chance to stop by our booth, too, before the presentations start."

The judge peered at Mr. Farley's name tag.

"Farley, eh? That's right. The computer, isn't it?"

Mr. Farley's face lit up. "Yes, that's us. Last year's state champions."

"A very impressive display. Very." Farley allowed himself a modest simper and was about to speak when the judge added, "And the kids did it all themselves, did they?"

"Oh, yes, sir," said Wilton Pflummerfield. "We did. All of it. Ourselves."

"Even the gigabyte interface?"

"Uh, sure," said Wilton. "Even the, um, the giggly-bit thing, right, Ralph?"

"Yeah," said Ralph. "The giggly-bit part was easy."

The judge nodded thoughtfully. "I found the computer very impressive, as I said. Perhaps the most impressive display I'd seen." Mr. Farley started to say something about how hard the class had worked on it, when he noticed the judge's attention wandering. He was looking again at the poster of the Egg Machine.

"But now *this*," said the judge, "*this* is something I've never seen before."

Julie dug her elbow into Simon's ribs. "Hey!" she whispered. "He likes it."

Much as Simon wanted to believe her, he was only too aware that the judge's comment could be taken two entirely different ways.

142

Ace in the Hole

"I can't believe it," said Otis Lister, pacing up and down in the auditorium hallway. "Is it really possible that that old woman and those, those ignoramus students can have made something that will win the Science Fair?"

"It seems impossible," said Mr. Farley. "But—"

"I wrote every member of the school board and informed them about the problem with Mrs. Maxwell and Bickle's refusal to fire her. Then I invited them all to the Science Fair and told them how you would bring honor to the school by winning it, hands down. They're expecting you to win, Charley. If *she* wins, we both look like fools. And Mr. Bickle's job is secure for another year."

"You have to stop her," said Farley.

"Correction," said Mr. Lister. "*We* have to stop her. I have an ace in the hole." He pulled a piece of paper out of his coat pocket. "I was hoping I wouldn't need to use it. But just in case it doesn't work, I need you to do what you can. *Whatever* you can. Do you catch my drift?"

"Yes," said Farley grimly. "Yes, I catch your drift."

"Good. Now please tell Mrs. Maxwell that I need to speak to her urgently."

Mr. Lister met Matilda outdoors by the teeter-totters. Mattie did not arrive promptly, of course, and Mr. Lister was fidgeting nervously by the time she did arrive.

"What is it, dear?" asked Mrs. Maxwell. "Where's the fire?"

"No fire," said Mr. Lister, pulling the paper slowly from his coat. "I just need to ask you—"

"Of course," said Mattie. "Ask away."

"I need you—"

"Excuse me," said Mattie. "But your shoelace is untied. So dangerous, an untied lace."

Mr. Lister flushed and tied his shoe. He stood up. He straightened his tie. He cleared his throat. At last he spoke. "You must withdraw your entry in the Science Fair."

Matilda was flabbergasted. "Why should I do that?"

"It has come to my attention that you have not completed the necessary paperwork—permission forms and so on. You will remember I gave them to you some time ago. If the judges find out, which they will, you must be disqualified."

Matilda broke into a smile. "Oh, if that's all," she said. Then she bent over her enormous purse and began to empty its contents onto the ground. Out came a fold-up umbrella, one left shoe, a telephone book for Schenectady, New York, a bag of carrots, a bag of parrot food, two screwdrivers (regular and Phillips head), a bag of

144

porcupine quills, a bag of feathers, a back scratcher, Band-Aids, butterscotch candy, and finally a bulging manila folder. She removed a handful of papers.

"Here they are," she said, thrusting them at Mr. Lister. "Contract for Science Fair Behavior." He looked at them, unsmiling, and read each one carefully.

"Yes. They appear to be all here." He gave her a thin smile. "However, I still must insist that you withdraw your entry. You needn't concern yourself with the reason."

Matilda stared at him. "Why would I do that?"

"If you wish to keep your job. You see, Mrs. Maxwell, you do things in a most unorthodox manner. That may work on a farm, but in a school, we must do things in the correct and orderly way. Chaos has no place in a school. We have policies and rules, and you have broken almost every rule I can think of." He read from the paper he was holding. "Administering medicine without a consent form—"

"An aspirin?"

"Quite illegal, as I told you. Then this matter of bringing animals into the classroom—"

"Runcible?"

"The school board has a firm policy on that. Putting student lives in danger, you know."

"A life-threatening parrot?"

"Allergies, Mrs. Maxwell. Allergies are no laughing matter. Therefore, a strict no-pets policy."

"But Runcible is not a pet. She was part of a science experiment: the feather and the quill. Besides, no one in the class has parrot allergies."

"Nonetheless, the school policy is quite clear."

Matilda sighed. She pulled out the folder again and handed the whole thing to Mr. Lister.

"What's all this, then?" he asked, shuffling through the mass of paperwork. "What on earth is all this?"

"Papers. Forms. Permission slips. What-have-you. I think you'll find it's all there, as requested. Plus a few others I threw in myself, just to be on the safe side."

Mr. Lister picked up a sheet at random. "What's this? I never requested this. Permission to Administer Spelling Test? And this? Consent Form for Vocabulary

Lessons? Extracurricular Policy for Cookies and Lemonade?"

"Yes, many of the parents were dismayed by all the paperwork, but I assured them that this was the way Mr. Lister liked things done. I think you'll find the aspirin forms are there as well. And all the others you wanted."

"They had better be complete. If just one is missing, it is enough to get you fired. And just between you and I, it is quite easy to fire substitutes. I'm giving you one last—"

" 'You and *me.*' "

"Hunh?"

" 'Just between you and *me.*' Grammar, Mr. Lister." Matilda looked down at her hands for a minute. "I would be sad to leave my students," she said. "I have enjoyed them very much."

"Are you telling me that you will not withdraw your entry?"

"I can't, Mr. Lister. Even if I wanted to. It's not really *my* entry. It is entirely the children's. They thought it up. They made it."

"Then Monday could be your last day here, you understand that?"

"If that's the way it has to be. Good day, Mr. Lister."

"Think it over, Mrs. Maxwell," he called after her. "You have half an hour to change your mind."

Fowl Play

batteries ✓
music ✓
remote control ✓
guinea pig ✓
guinea hen ✓

Where was Aunt Mattie? Simon glanced at the clock over the door. It was the same kind of round, white clock you saw in every gymnasium you went into. It said 12:40. Twenty minutes to one. Only thirty-five minutes until the time to present to the judges.

Nor was Uncle Philbert anywhere to be seen. He had been dispatched to find an extra extension cord (really it was just an excuse to keep him away from the Egg Machine). And a kind of controlled pandemonium was in progress at the class's booth. Mindy and Mandy were going over final changes in the speech they had written for the presentation. Julie, who was to read the speech, was walking up and down practicing it, accompanying it with many dramatic hand gestures. Mollie was checking batteries. And other students were adding the last touches to the poster or to the Egg Machine itself. After the judge made his comments, a kind of panicky hope had filled the students—the possibility, the actual possibility that they might win the Science Fair. Even Simon, against his better judgment, found himself catching the excitement. Who knows, he thought. Ever since Aunt Mattie with her outlandish ways had blown into his life, everything he had ever taken for granted had been turned upside down. Maybe this would be, too.

"Listen," said Sebastian, once everything had been assembled. "Let's run through the checklist, to be sure we're all ready to go. It's getting late."

"But Aunt—Mrs. Maxwell's not back," said Simon. Where *was* she?

"We don't need her," said Julie. "And I know she'd agree." The students began to run through the list: Batteries? Check. Music? Check. Remote control? Check. Guinea pig? Check. Guinea hen?

No answer.

"Guinea hen? Raggie?"

There was a shout from under the table. It was Raggie. He stood up and looked around in panic.

"What is it?" asked Mindy.

"It's Henrietta," Raggie said. "She's gone."

Sabotage

"What do you mean, gone? Did she escape from the box? Come on, we can find her," said Mindy.

"No," said Raggie. "Really gone. The whole box and everything. Someone must've took her."

Total silence fell as the students realized the extent of the disaster. No hen. No eggs. Therefore no Egg Machine. Finally Raggie said what everyone was thinking.

"Sabotage."

The students all began talking at once.

"I knew it!"

"Yeah, it's those creeps from Mr. Farley's class. I saw them messing around behind the table about fifteen minutes ago. They'd do anything to win—even cheat."

"They kidnapped our hen!"

"What'll we do?"

"Shouldn't we wait for Mrs. Maxwell?" asked Simon.

"There isn't time," said Jimmy. "Let's go get Henny back!"

"Wait a minute," said Simon. "Raggie, you run over to Mr. Farley's booth and ask if anyone has seen

Henrietta. Maybe someone picked up her box by mistake."

"Yeah," muttered Mario under his breath. "Like they mistook her for a box of Chicken Nuggets."

Raggie was back in two minutes. "They all say they haven't seen her," he panted. He didn't add that any three-year-old could have told that they were lying.

"Sure," said Julie. "What did you expect?" Everyone nodded, and an angry, glum silence descended.

"What're we gonna do?" moaned Mindy.

"All this work, and for nothing," said Jimmy. He kicked a table leg. "I say we all march over there together, right now, and demand that they give Henrietta back. Tell them we'll smash their computer if they don't."

There was a chorus of agreement. Jimmy picked up a hammer. So did Ethan. "Let's go!" they said.

"Wait!" said Simon, looking around desperately for his aunt. "This isn't what Mrs. Maxwell would want us to do."

"How do you know what she would want?" growled Jimmy. He was still clutching his hammer.

"I just do," said Simon.

"Simon's right," said Julie. "Mrs. Maxwell would say something like"—and she put on her best, crisp Aunt Mattie voice—" 'You know very well that violence solves nothing.' "

Her imitation of Aunt Mattie was so convincing that a collective sigh of disappointment ran through the class. Jimmy put down his hammer. So did Ethan.

There was another long silence. Simon looked at the clock. It was ten to one. Time was running out. Then Raggie stepped forward.

"Violence isn't right," said little Raggie, and Simon wanted to shake his hand. Then he went on. "But there's another way to sabotage it—a nonviolent way. And they'll never guess we did it."

"How?"

Raggie looked around at the group with his crooked grin. "We have a secret weapon," he said.

Everyone looked at him blankly. Just then Philbert showed up at a trot, out of breath and clutching a bright orange extension cord.

"I found a cord," he announced. "But danged if I can get it to work."

Her What?

"What?" said Philbert, looking around. "What is it? Why is everyone staring at me? Don't you know it's rude to stare? It's not my fault the danged cord won't work. The janitor told me—"

"Oh, we don't need that cord, Mr. Maxwell," said Julie, stepping forward. "Here, let me have it." She dropped it onto a table. "But we were just kind of wondering if, um, if you had ever used a computer before. Wouldn't you like to try out a computer? Mr. Farley's class has this really neat one at their booth."

"Yeah," chimed in Jimmy. "It's really cool."

"Me?" said Philbert. "Now what use would I have for a computer? I hate the dang things. I can add and subtract perfectly well with a pencil, thank you very much. No, I—"

"Please," said Julie, giving him her most winning smile. "Right now. You have to hurry, because in a few minutes it will be too late."

The class had closed in around Philbert and were slowly propelling him down the gymnasium toward

Mr. Farley's booth, talking quickly as they went. Simon knew what they were up to. All it would take would be a few seconds, just long enough for Uncle Philbert to lay his hands on the computer. Heck, probably all he had to do was look at it and the logic boards would go up in smoke. Simon glanced again at the clock: 12:55. In five minutes, Mr. Farley's class would be giving their presentation to the judges, and it would be too late. Already a small crowd had begun to gather in front of Mr. Farley's booth to view the presentation. He hated to do this, but he had to.

"Stop!"

The lynch mob, if you can call a group of computer slayers a lynch mob, turned and stared at Simon. Simon pushed his way to the front and pulled Philbert away from the mob. "Uncle Philbert," he whispered urgently into his ear, "I need you to go get Aunt Mattie. Right away." Philbert stared. He wasn't used to being issued orders by young whippersnappers, but something in Simon's tone convinced him. He nodded and, with a backward glance at the class, vanished to search for his wife.

"Why'd you do that?" yelled Jimmy angrily. "He was about to do what we wanted."

"Shut up, Jimmy," said Simon. "You know—everyone here knows—it would have been wrong—just as wrong as smashing it with a hammer. Mrs. Maxwell would never have let us get away with that, ever."

Jimmy was still angry. Simon could practically see him forming the thought—Goody-goody!—in his mind. "Yeah," Jimmy taunted him, "so who made you the instant expert on what Mrs. Maxwell thinks? Are you her special pet or something?"

"No," said Simon. He glanced over the faces of the members of his class. Then he took a deep breath and said, "I'm her nephew." This news was greeted with silent stupefaction by all but Julie. Julie shook her head and started laughing.

"Her what?" said Jimmy at last.

"Her great-nephew, actually," said Simon. "And as her great-nephew, I can promise you that if you don't stop trying to sabotage Mr. Farley's class, she'll . . . she'll *gashiate* your *corporosity* when she gets back. So let's find another plan."

There was no time for anyone to discuss Simon's amazing revelation, for it was only too clear that he was right. They had to quickly find another solution. Then, just when things looked the bleakest, Aunt Mattie finally showed up, out of breath, trailing Uncle Philbert. She had a funny look on her face, a look Simon had never seen before. A look that he could only describe as fierce.

As the students filled her in on the disaster, she shook her head several times. But all she said was, "Well, what do you think we should do now? Time's a-wasting."

There was a long and painful silence. At last Mollie raised her hand.

"I guess maybe we could run to a store or something and try to buy some eggs," she said, without a lot of enthusiasm.

"Now you're thinking," said Matilda. But her words were greeted with a gloomy silence.

"Store eggs are boring," said Mindy. "Henrietta's eggs were so nice and round."

"Besides, there isn't time," said Mario. "If we're even a minute late, we get disqualified."

"Never mind," said Matilda. "That's not what's important. Perhaps we won't be allowed to win a ribbon, but I'm sure the judges will still let us do our presentation, and that's what counts. Winning would be gratifying, I'm sure, but the main thing is to show them what we can do. The main thing is the Mighty Muculent Egg Machine. And unless anyone has any other ideas, that's what we'll do. Now, whose parents could go fetch some eggs for us?" A dozen hands were glumly raised.

Raggie looked at Jimmy in surprise. "Your family is here?" he asked. "I thought they only went to basketball recitals, or whatever they're called."

"Yeah, well, that's because I promised them we were going to win."

"Winning isn't everything," continued Matilda. "As my old granny used to say—"

But what her old granny used to say will remain forever a mystery, for it was at that exact moment that Runcible chose to join the discussion.

"Cluck," she said from her cage under the table. "Cluck. Cluck. Cluck."

Runcible to the Rescue

Cluck?

Simon looked at Jimmy. Jimmy looked at Raggie. In fact, everyone looked at everyone else with an expression that the poet Keats would undoubtedly have described as "wild surmise," rather like Cortez's men did when they stood silent on that peak in Darien and for the first time cast their eyes upon the noble Pacific Ocean.

Unlike Cortez's men, however, Simon and his classmates did not stand silent, not for long anyway.

"Runcible!" they clamored. "Runcible! Mrs. Maxwell, do parrots lay eggs? Do they? Is Runcible a girl or a boy? Could she lay an egg? Has she ever laid an egg?"

Matilda looked at Philbert.

"Once," he said. "In 1973. It was a lovely green egg, too. Kinda small. I convinced her not to try again, though. They can't hatch, you see."

"Could she lay an egg for us today, though?"

Philbert stroked his long silver mustache thoughtfully.

"Not likely," he said. "Would take a miracle. Unless

maybe Henrietta has been giving her lessons. Who knows? How much time do we have?"

"About twenty minutes. More, if we can stall."

"Well, no harm tryin'. I'll go have a word with her."

And so Philbert put Runcible in the nesting box that perched atop the Egg Machine and sat down to have a long talk with her, while overhead the hands of the clock crept closer and closer to 1:15.

Cabotinage

At precisely 1:15, the judges headed for the Mighty Muculent Egg Machine exhibit. Behind them were students, and behind them, parents, teachers, and other curious onlookers. They were talking eagerly to each other, but not about the Egg Machine. No, they were talking about Mr. Farley's computer demonstration, which they had just witnessed. Simon's few glimmers of hope were instantly replaced with gloom. All he could hear were comments about how astonishing, how clever, kids these days, isn't it amazing, imagine building a *real computer*. The only one not exclaiming about the computer was the judge who'd stopped by their booth earlier. Simon stared at him, trying hard to believe that the expression on his face was one of disbelief and skepticism. It *could* be. On the other hand—and this is what Simon feared was true—it could also be disbelief and *amazement*.

At last the judges formed a ring around the Egg Machine, and one gave the signal to commence. Mindy stood up.

"We would like to introduce the Mighty Muculent Egg-Breaking and Breakfast-Making Morning-Waking Machine," she began, but she was instantly interrupted by a judge.

"Excuse me," he said. "I don't wish to appear ignorant, but perhaps you could tell us what muculent means?"

"Oh, sure. It means like slimy. We could've said slimy, I guess, but muculent sounded better."

"Quite right," said the judge, and others nodded their heads in agreement. "Proceed."

"Okay." She gave a nervous look over at the Egg Machine. All that was visible of it behind the curtain was Uncle Philbert's head and Runcible, sitting in her nest box, uncharacteristically silent. Philbert was talking to her. The store eggs had not shown up yet. "First I'd like to explain that usually we have a guinea hen here but due to nefarious—"

But Matilda was shaking her head at her and whispering, "No excuses."

"—um, nefarious circumstances beyond our control, we are using a parrot. And we hope it works." She looked back at her notes. "We decided to invent the Egg Machine because nobody, at least none of us, likes to get up in the morning and have to make breakfast feeling all sleepy. So the Egg Machine lets you sleep in while your breakfast is made for you, and then it wakes you up nicely. And your breakfast is all done. It's kind of fun. And we all worked on it, together, each person did. Just us. No grown-ups."

Simon saw the judges smiling and nodding in agreement. He knew that Mindy was playing for time, but the judges didn't seem to care. Mindy looked at the gymnasium door. Still no sign of the store eggs. How much longer could she stall?

"I definitely need one of those," said one judge to another.

"We decided to use a guinea hen because it was kind of inspired by that Dr. Seuss book, *Scrambled Eggs Super,* and it seemed more interesting than regular eggs. I really love that book, don't you?" Mindy was just making stuff up now. She glanced again at the gymnasium door.

"Very literary," said another judge. Several judges laughed, but Simon saw another one frown and look at her watch.

"We need to proceed," she said. "We have many more presentations to hear."

"Right," said Mindy. "Well, we all came up with some stuff and then we built it all by ourselves from plans, and here it is," she finished hurriedly and lamely. "And Julie will explain how it works."

Julie stood up and, using a wooden pointer, gestured toward the hidden Egg Machine.

"Ladies and gentlemen," she said dramatically, talking in the sing-song voice of a carnival showman, "let me introduce to you the one, the only, Mighty Muculent Egg-Breaking and Breakfast-Making Morning-Waking Machine!"

She nodded to Bix and Ethan, who pulled the ropes and opened the curtain that had screened the Egg Machine from view. There it stood, a strange Rube

Goldberg contraption topped with a nest box, in which Runcible the parrot sat looking self-important. Some yards behind it, lying on a table and snoring loudly, was Mario, pretending to be fast asleep.

The crowd laughed, and at that precise instant, Runcible gave a loud squawk, ruffled her wings, and said, unmistakably, "Cluck!" She stood up, sat down, and looked around with a proud and somewhat startled expression in her eyes. Somewhat like those men on the peak in Darien.

Philbert bent over the nest box, stood up, and flashed Julie a huge grin, his thumb and finger making the okay sign. A vast sigh of relief escaped from all of Matilda's students, as well as some cheers and clapping. Simon cheered louder than anyone. Runcible had come through. Great-uncle Philbert and good old Runcible had come through.

"You go, girl!" said Julie happily, and then she seemed to recollect where she was. She put on her serious face. "Yes, the Mighty Egg Machine: It shakes, it bakes, *and* it wakes you up! And at the same time it demonstrates how science can make our lives better, using only the forces of nature—gravity, heat, jet propulsion, laser beams, and shall we say *alternative* forms of energy.

"We start with, as Mindy explained, the simple guinea hen, Latin name *Numida meleagris*." She looked up from her note cards. "Or, uh, in this case the parrot. Latin name, um, *Parrotosis thingummi*." The judges laughed again. Good, thought Simon. Go, Julie.

"Each morning, or perhaps during the night, the hen

will lay an egg in the nest box." She pointed to the nest box with the pointer. "The egg remains in the box until, at a preset time, this nasty alarm clock goes off, startling the hen so that she jumps out of the nest box."

Just then a loud buzzing erupted under the nest box, and Runcible jumped squawking onto Philbert's shoulder.

"Oh, my sainted aunt!" said the parrot. "Shut up!"

Julie continued, trying not to laugh. "The change in weight releases a spring on a trapdoor in the bottom of the nest box, allowing the egg to roll out down this ramp made of Lego pieces"—and indeed, as she spoke, a small green egg could be seen rolling lopsidedly down the ramp. All the students cheered—they couldn't help themselves—at the sight of that lovely little egg.

"Way to go, Runcible!"

CLUCK!

The Mighty Muculent Egg-Breaking and Breakfast-Making Morning-Waking Machine!

Julie resumed.

"The egg shoots off the end of the ramp, into the little basketball hoop, and lands in this strainer." As the egg shot off the ramp and passed perfectly through the small hoop, a voice from the crowd yelled, "Yo! A three-pointer!" Turning, Simon saw a boy in a high-school varsity jacket, who looked like a taller, older version of Jimmy, giving Jimmy a high five. Jimmy was blushing with pleasure.

"Well," continued Julie, "the strainer is really just a metal bowl we punched holes in. Of course, the egg gets smashed to smithereens, and all the egg stuff drips through the strainer, leaving the shells behind."

"Very clever," said one of the judges, and the grown-ups all applauded as the egg did just that.

"Now comes the part that will amaze and surprise you," said Julie, resuming her carnival voice. "The egg glop drips through the strainer into this mixing bowl with milk and salt and pepper, or whatever you like in it. You can put pancake mix in it if you like, or waffle mix.

"Meanwhile, the force of the egg landing on the strainer releases this carrot in the guinea-pig cage here."

"My guinea pig," interjected Mandy. "His name is Percy."

"Percy sees the carrot and tries to run after it on his treadmill. The treadmill turns the eggbeaters here, which beat up the egg and milk. You see—scrambled eggs! At the same time, the treadmill also winds up this rubber band attached to this wooden arm that holds the bowl, and when it gets too tight"—here she paused, waiting for the rubber band to stretch—"it snaps! Like that! And the arm pivots like so, dumping the contents of the bowl into this frying pan underneath it here.

"The other end of the wooden arm has a piece of flint attached to it which now smashes into this piece of flint here—"

"My flint—" said Jimmy.

"—causing a spark, which ignites this can of Sterno cooking fuel under the frying pan. The eggs start to cook." Julie turned to the crowd. *"Isn't that amazing?"* she said in her best cable TV infomercial voice. And the crowd responded—clapping and cheering— just like an infomercial crowd.

"Cool!" said a student from Mr. Farley's class.

"Shut up," hissed another student from the same class.

"A fire hazard," objected Mr. Lister. "Do they have a fire permit for this?"

"But what about the waking-up part?" asked a judge. "You said it woke you up nicely in time for breakfast."

Julie held up her hands dramatically. Silence fell on the crowd.

"Patience," said Julie. "All will be made clear. Keep your eyes on this string here."

Everyone watched as the flame of the Sterno lit a piece of string strung between the flame and the frying pan. Suddenly, the string hissed into life—it was actually a rocket fuse—and burned slowly until it ignited a little plastic rocket ship balanced on the low end of a small seesaw. The rocket flew straight up into the air, opened a parachute, and floated gently to the ground.

"The rocket ship is not important," said Julie in a

voice that sounded now exactly like the Wizard in *The Wizard of Oz.* "What's important is this." And she gestured to a machine behind the rocket-launching pad—a CD player that suddenly whirred into life.

"You see before you an example of the miracle of infrared light technology at work," explained Julie. "Yes, the high end of the seesaw was blocking the beam from this remote-control device here, which is aimed at the on/off switch of the CD player back there. And so, just at the precise moment when your eggs, your farm-fresh guinea-hen and parrot scrambled eggs super-de-dooper, when they're done cooking, the rocket ship takes off, the end of the seesaw drops down, and the remote beam now strikes the CD player behind it and turns it on. And"—there was a blast of ear-splitting rock and roll from a speaker next to the table Mario was lying on—"your favorite music is piped upstairs to a speaker in your bedroom, gently waking you just in time for breakfast."

Mario, who had either genuinely fallen asleep or done a perfect imitation of it, was now jolted awake with such force that he fell off the table onto the floor. He stumbled to his feet, rubbing his eyes, and the audience burst into laughter.

Julie turned to the crowd and, with perfect timing, concluded: "Ladies and gentlemen, I give you the world's first, the one and only Mighty Muculent Egg-Breaking and Breakfast-Making Morning-Waking Machine!" She took a sweeping bow and the entire room erupted into applause.

"Yes," said Mr. Farley, clapping very slowly and looking all around to see who might agree with him. "Yes, but is it science?"

The superintendent of schools, handing out awards at the end of the day, seemed to think so. Giving the first-place trophy to Mrs. Maxwell's class, he said he found the project "unique" and "original" and "unorthodox" as well as "highly practical." "When can I buy one?" he asked.

So, too, did the cheering parents and the two beaming members of the school board. "You did us proud today, Herbie," said one school-board member, slapping Mr. Bickle on the back. "You did the school proud."

Mr. Bickle smiled shyly. "Well, it was really... Mrs. Maxwell is the one who ... and of course the children are, too."

"Don't be so modest, Herbie." The other school-board member turned to Mr. Lister, who was trying to edge away from them unnoticed.

"There you are, Otis," he boomed. "What do you say to that, eh? Stroke of genius, hiring that woman, on such short notice, too. Don't you agree? Eh?"

"Oh, yes," said Mr. Lister with a nervous laugh. "Genius. It is a pleasure and a privilege to work for such a man as Mr. Bickle."

After the ceremony Simon and Julie slipped away to look for Henrietta. They found her sitting under the table in her box, next to Runcible's cage, as if she'd never left. While Julie picked up the guinea hen to see if she was okay, Simon opened Runcible's cage and let her sidestep up to his shoulder, where she sat, nibbling his ear and cooing affectionately.

"They must have returned Henny while we were up there getting our award," he said.

Julie looked at Simon and Runcible for a while. "You two look like old friends," she said.

Simon stroked Runcible. "We are," he said.

"Why didn't you say something, about her being your aunt and all?"

"I don't know. I wanted to, but the first day, it was too weird. I felt embarrassed. And then, the longer I waited, the harder it got."

Julie nodded. "Yeah," she said. "I can see that. So what changed your mind?"

"I kept thinking about what you said this morning, about believing in something, no matter how weird it looks to other people."

Once again Julie nodded. She was being unusually quiet. Then she said, in her typical, blunt way, "So what are you going to do about it? To make it up to her, I mean. You must feel pretty rotten. She doesn't know you told everyone just now."

"What *can* I do?" asked Simon miserably. "Stand up in front of the class? And what do I say?"

Julie was silent. She shrugged. It was Runcible, as usual, who piped up.

"Say thank you," said the parrot. "Say you're sorry." She tugged on Simon's hair with her beak. "Get over it."

Badinage

Monday morning. Matilda was late. Simon was writing on the blackboard, and the others were standing around, watching him and talking animatedly.

"They can't fire her now, can they?" said Mindy. "Not after winning the Science Fair."

"Yeah," said Mollie. "We gotta go to the States."

Ethan shrugged. "Hey, I'm just telling you what I heard some of Mr. Farley's kids saying. Grown-ups can do anything they want. It doesn't have to make sense."

Simon interrupted. "Let's try it one more time," he said, pointing to the board. But at that moment the door opened and Jimmy dragged Raggie back into the classroom. Raggie had been standing guard for Mrs. Maxwell, and Jimmy had been standing guard over Raggie. "She's coming!" cried Raggie. Simon looked out the door. In the corridor he could see Mrs. Maxwell and Mr. Lister, deep in conversation. Everyone else ran to their seats.

When Matilda opened the door, the room was completely quiet. The students rose slowly to their feet. They stood there, all grinning and looking expectantly at her.

She placed Runcible's cage on the floor and went to her desk. The students remained standing. Simon stayed put. Matilda looked at them quizzically.

"Good morning," she said, at last. "And how does your corporosity seem to gashiate today?" She began to delve into her purse.

There was a pause, then, at a signal from Simon, everyone answered in unison:

"*Very discombobulate. Great congruity. Dissimilarity.*"

And then they sat down.

Matilda looked from Simon to the students, and back to Simon. A smile creased her face.

"Thank you, class. You may sit down now, Simon."

"Yes, Aunt Mattie," he said.

She smiled again at the words *Aunt Mattie.* Then she addressed Julie.

"By the way, my dear," she said, "it's *corporosity.*"

"Huh?" said Julie.

"*Corporosity.* Not *porporosity*: 'How does your *corporosity* seem to *gashiate.*'"

"Oh," said Julie. "Right. *Corporosity.*"

There was a silence. Then Jimmy stood up. "Mrs. Maxwell?" he said.

"Yes, dear?"

"They aren't really going to fire you, are they?"

Matilda looked around the classroom again. She looked at the front of the room, where the students had strung all their blue ribbons across the blackboard. She looked at the words Simon had written there: "very discombobulate, great congruity, dissimilarity." She looked at Simon.

"I am glad to see that you have learned *something* from my time here," she said, ignoring the question. And Simon couldn't tell if she was talking to the class, or just to him. "One might even say we had spent our time most—"

"Proficuously?" interjected Raggie.

Matilda smiled. "Precisely. I couldn't have put it better myself. But enough badinage. We have important work to do. After all, we are going to the State Science Fair."

The children cheered. And then from her pockets she produced the familiar porcupine quill, parrot feather, and magnifying glass. "Now children," said Matilda, "the quill—"

"What? You don't know what a whiffet is? Tarnation! What are they teaching you kids, anyway?"

Uncle Philbert's glossary

badinage: joking talk, banter

cabotinage: hamming it up for dramatic effect

jackanape: saucy or mischievous child

miscreant: someone who behaves badly; a criminal

muculent: slimy

nefarious: wicked

pecksniffian: selfish and corrupt while trying to seem friendly and kind

persiflage: lying

proficuous: profitable, useful

quisling: traitor

rodomontade: a bragging, vain, or boastful speech

whiffet: small, young, or unimportant person

MacDonald, Amy
No More Nasty.

DATE DUE	BORROWER'S NAME